"If you behave yourself, there won't be any problems..."

Teagan shook off her somber mood. "What fun is it to behave myself?"

Chase breathed a sigh of relief at her quicksilver return to flirting. Serious, reflective Teagan was dangerous to his self-preservation. "Maybe if you don't meddle with your family, we could avoid future disagreements."

"But then you wouldn't be tasked to keep an eye on me." Her palm made contact with his thigh. "And I think you like what's happening between us."

Her touch was no more settling this time around. In fact, he was finding it difficult to concentrate on anything except for his thundering pulse. With the urge to kiss her growing too sharp to ignore, he set his fingers beneath her chin and coaxed her closer.

"It pains me to say this." He brushed her lips with his. Excitement sparked at the glancing touch and he savored the sweet pain. "But you might be right..."

* * *

The Trouble with Love and Hate by Cat Schield is part of the Sweet Tea and Scandal series.

Dear Reader,

This Sweet Tea and Scandal series set in Charleston, South Carolina, has been such an amazing ride and I'm sad to see it end. This final book was challenging to write. My heroine was the villain of the previous story and I've never tackled a redemption story before. Plus, the hero I intended for her was definitely not Mr. Right. So, I went back to the drawing board and came up with the perfect man for her.

Once again, I hope I've done Charleston justice. I adore the city although I've never visited. It is definitely on my bucket list of places to go. I love the historic charm and imagine myself happily eating my way through dozens of restaurants.

The Trouble with Love and Hate is an enemies-to-lovers tale, one of my favorite tropes. I hope you enjoy watching Teagan and Chase find their way to happily-ever-after.

Happy reading,

Cat Schield

CAT SCHIELD

THE TROUBLE WITH
LOVE AND HATE

HARLEQUIN®
DESIRE™

Recycling programs
for this product may
not exist in your area.

ISBN-13: 978-1-335-58159-4

The Trouble with Love and Hate

Harlequin Enterprises ULC
22 Adelaide St. West, 41st Floor
Toronto, Ontario M5H 4E3, Canada
www.Harlequin.com

Printed in U.S.A.

Cat Schield is an award-winning author of contemporary romances for Harlequin Desire. She likes her heroines spunky and her heroes swoonworthy. While her jet-setting characters live all over the globe, Cat makes her home in Minnesota with her daughter, two opinionated Burmese cats and a goofy Doberman. When she's not writing or walking dogs, she's searching for the perfect cocktail or traveling to visit friends and family. Contact her at www.catschield.com.

Books by Cat Schield

Harlequin Desire

Sweet Tea and Scandal

Upstairs Downstairs Baby
Substitute Seduction
Revenge with Benefits
Seductive Secrets
Seduction, Southern Style
The Trouble with Love and Hate

Texas Cattleman's Club: Ranchers and Rivals

On Opposite Sides

Visit her Author Profile page at Harlequin.com, or catschield.com, for more titles!

You can also find Cat Schield on Facebook, along with other Harlequin Desire authors, at Facebook.com/harlequindesireauthors!

For Robin Selvig.

One

Chase Love sat on the couch in his office, his two-year-old niece asleep on his lap. Her older sister lay on the floor near his feet, her forehead puckered in concentration as she plied bright crayons to her favorite coloring book.

At the conference table across the room, real estate agent Sawyer Thurston was on her cell phone, trying once again to negotiate a deal with Chase's irascible third cousin. A decade earlier Rufus Calloway had inherited a tumbledown Charleston house that had sentimental value to Chase's mother. Since then, Maybelle Love had been trying to convince her estranged cousin to sell the abandoned property.

"I don't care how much they're offering!" Rufus's enraged voice came through the cell phone's speaker loud and clear. "That family is never going to get their hands on my property."

After the declaration, Rufus must've put an end to the conversation because Sawyer lowered the phone and blew out a weary breath. "Well, that's a hard no."

"Yeah."

Sensing business was done for the moment, four-year-old Annabelle was a blond streak as she sprang off the floor and skipped toward Sawyer. "Look what I colored."

"Wow!" Chase's longtime friend crouched to admire the drawing. "That's really beautiful. When you're done with it, may I put it up in my office?"

"Oh, yes." Always pleased to have her artwork praised, Annabelle carried the coloring book back to the box of crayons on the floor.

While his niece returned to her art, Sawyer made her way toward him. To accommodate the muggy July temperatures, the slender brunette wore a sleeveless white blouse and bright floral skirt.

"What's our next step?" Chase asked, indicating the empty cushion beside him.

Sawyer settled onto the sofa, glanced at the sleeping child and shot him a look of grim determination. "Rufus is not going to sell the property to anyone in your family."

"I'm not ready to give up."

"I know. It's just that rumor has it his financial situation has gotten worse. He's going to sell the property to someone and it's not going to be anyone in your family. That being said, I might have a buyer who would satisfy both Rufus and your mom."

Chase hated the idea that the Calloway property would slip through his family's fingers, but Rufus was holding all the cards. "My mom wants the house restored to its former glory. If we can't buy the property, it's important that the buyer understands the home's historic significance. It will destroy her if the home is torn down and a modern monstrosity gets built in its place."

"I know." Sawyer shot him an exasperated look. They'd had this conversation so many times over the years. "This person is keen to renovate a historic property. As soon as I found out Rufus was going to sell, I got in touch with her and told her all about it." Sawyer's real estate focus was primarily on historical properties and she frequently brought clients to East Bay Construction, the renovation and construction company owned by Chase and his partner Knox Poole. "I explained that you've done all the preliminary work getting the architectural plans ready and figuring out what structural work needs to happen to bring the buildings up to code. She's really excited to work with you."

"You already talked to someone?" Chase wasn't happy with this development, but he appreciated Sawyer's pragmatism. Their mother was dead set on owning the property and stubbornly refused to consider any options. "Who is it?"

"Someone new to the area," Sawyer said, and seeing Chase's frown, rushed to add, "but with strong ties to one of Charleston's oldest families."

Something about Sawyer's caginess sparked concern. "Who is it?" He repeated the question with soft menace.

"Teagan Burns." Sawyer actively avoided meeting his gaze as she spoke.

"Ethan's cousin?" Chase was stunned by the suggestion. Ever since showing up in Charleston last month, the New York socialite had been making trouble for Chase's best friend, Ethan Watts. "Absolutely not."

"Oh, come on. She's the exact sort of client you love to work with. Passionate about restoration." Dimples flashed in Sawyer's cheeks as she added in a coaxing tone, "Unlimited funds."

Chase ignored Sawyer's teasing, unwilling to even consider her suggestion. "You neglected to add drama-free," he prompted.

"I found her to be sensible, smart and quite likable. And I've already pitched her you as her partner on the project."

Unconvinced, Chase shook his head. "That will never work."

"Come on." The enthusiasm in Sawyer's blue-gray eyes took on greater fervor. "She's smart, ambitious and knows exactly what she wants."

"You sound like you feel sorry for her."

"She made a mistake. I don't think she's a terrible person. You know why she's interested in the Calloway property, right?"

"Because she wants to renovate a historic house."

"And provide transition homes for women leaving domestic abuse situations."

Leave it to Sawyer to hit him where he was most vulnerable. For many years, his older sister had been in an abusive relationship. She'd done an excellent job hiding the situation from her family and Chase had never forgiven himself for missing the signs. When at last Nola had managed to escape her situation, she'd had her family to turn to. Not all women were as lucky.

"It's why she's been looking for multi-family prop-erties," Sawyer continued. "I've shown her several buildings and homes around downtown Charleston, but the Calloway house was the first one that fired her imagination."

"So she's seen it?" The poor condition of the turn-of-the-century Victorian had been scaring off buyers for a decade.

"Just the listing photos. I'm showing her the property in a bit." Sawyer leaned forward. "I know you and your mom are dying to have a say in how the main house is restored and Teagan wants to do some good in the community. It's a win-win for everyone."

"All I see is a scheming troublemaker who intends to manipulate things to make herself look better." Chase couldn't imagine accepting Teagan as a client. "And I don't trust her not to cause my mother more distress."

"I am convinced she recognizes how badly she screwed up and will be honest and straightforward from now on."

Chase shook his head. "I'm not sure she can help herself. Look how she schemed to muscle in on Ethan's position at Watts Shipping and tried to involve her sister in the scheme."

"She admitted that was a huge miscalculation. I'm convinced that she came to Charleston determined to fit in with her biological family and misjudged how close the Wattses are and how they rally around each other. She's devastated that everyone is so mad at her."

Ethan's family had been looking for the missing Watts heiress for years and had finally found her after a genetic testing service had connected the biological relatives. Her arrival in Charleston had been greatly anticipated; however, she hadn't turned out to be all they'd hoped.

From what Chase had heard from his best friend, Teagan wasn't interested in developing a relationship with her Charleston family. Instead, she'd set her sights on being named the next CEO of the family's company, Watts Shipping, a position Ethan had expected would be his one day. In order to do this, she'd had to distract her cousin from figuring out what she was up to. Teagan had encouraged the attraction between Ethan and her adoptive sister, never imagining the pair would actually fall in love, or that Sienna would choose to take Ethan's side.

"You should at least hear her out before rejecting the idea," Sawyer said.

Chase wasn't convinced. "How did you two meet?"

"Through Poppy not long after Teagan arrived in town. Way before everything with Ethan blew up." Poppy Shaw was Ethan's cousin. It spoke to how badly Teagan had mucked up with her Charleston relations that Poppy, a free spirit with a forgiving nature, refused to stick up for her. "I've shown her a bunch of houses that need restoration, but none of them were quite right for her needs. I think the Calloway property would be perfect."

Despite the crushing disappointment at not being able to secure the house for his mother, Chase could see the potential in finding a buyer eager to bring the historic home back to its former glory. But not Teagan Burns. The partnership would aggravate his best friend and Chase couldn't trust her altruistic motives.

"No."

Sawyer narrowed her eyes. "Why?"

"Because she's from New York City."

The real estate agent released an exasperated breath. "What does that have to do with anything?"

"This is my family's house we're talking about. She won't be able to appreciate the history—"

"There are plenty of historic buildings in New York."

"Buildings they're tearing down to make way for modern skyscrapers."

"You haven't even met the woman. Why not at least hear her out?" When he didn't immediately refuse, Sawyer's expression grew calculated. "I'm meeting her in fifteen minutes at the house."

It was looking like whether or not he was on board, Teagan Burns might become the owner of the Calloway property. Grinding his teeth, Chase pondered the sleeping child draped across his legs and the one with the tip of her tongue stuck out as she colored a cartoon alligator. What was he supposed to do with his nieces? Nola wouldn't be back to pick up her daughters for at least another hour.

"Bring them along," Sawyer said, reading his mind.

Chase grunted. "To a business meeting?"

"So, now it's a business meeting?" Sawyer looked pleased. "That means you're actually considering working with Teagan on the project."

Was he? More likely, she would take one look at the ramshackle Victorian and reject it out of hand. The condition of the house and scope of the project would intimidate even the most experienced developer. He doubted the transplanted socialite would have the gumption to tackle a full restoration. Which meant the house's future was in jeopardy.

"It means," Chase grumbled, "I'm committed to saving my mother's ancestral home."

A bold statement, but his disquiet about Teagan persisted as he eased to the curb fifteen minutes later before the house owned by Rufus Calloway. Its position, directly across John Street from Chase's home, offered a constant reminder of the bad blood between the two branches of his family. Five years prior, Chase had purchased his historic "single house" fixer-upper and begun its transformation, hoping that Rufus would see the fine work being done and sell Chase his rundown Victorian. Unfortunately, his third cousin wasn't about to give up on the grudge that had twisted his family for a hundred years.

A white metallic Mercedes SUV sat before the property. On the sidewalk side of the vehicle stood a willowy blonde woman with her back to him.

Teagan Burns.

Although she'd been in Charleston for many weeks, Chase hadn't had time to meet her. Too many renovation projects needed completion to be entered into the city's annual Carolopolis Awards. And considering how poorly the socialite had treated his best friend, Chase was glad he hadn't wasted his time on her.

Now, if he wanted to do right by his mother's ancestral home, it looked like he wasn't going to have a choice.

With his jaw locked, Chase took her in. A sleeveless cream-colored dress skimmed her slender curves while a large designer bag, handles nestled in the crook of her left elbow, drew attention to her toned arms. Beachy waves of golden locks cascaded to her waist. Polished and sophisticated, she looked out of place in front of the weathered, gray structure.

Four-year-old Annabelle had fallen asleep during the ten-minute drive and grumbled as Chase lifted her out of her car seat and set her on her feet. In contrast, Hazel had been revived by her earlier nap and was raring to go.

Sawyer had not yet arrived as Chase made his way across the street—flanked by his nieces—and approached the New Yorker. "Ms. Burns?"

Teagan turned at the sound of her name and her eyes widened as she took Chase in. Something primal and alluring flared in her eyes, and for a moment his awareness of the street and his nieces fell away.

"I'm Chase Love."

"Well, hello." Her breathless greeting and dazzling smile left him momentarily blindsided.

Although Ethan had shown him pictures of Teagan Burns when it first came to light that she was the long-lost daughter of his aunt Ava, those images didn't have the impact of seeing Teagan's beauty in person.

"Sawyer Thurston is a business associate of mine. When she mentioned that you were interested in the Calloway property, she thought it would be good if I was here for the walk-through since I know it so well."

Since his name triggered no recognition, he'd left out his connection to Ethan. If they ended up working together in the future, he would have to deal with that problem then.

"Of course. Your company has a wonderful reputation when it comes to historic renovations. I look forward to hearing your evaluation." She cocked her head and glanced at his nieces. "And who are these two?"

"I'm Annabelle and this is my sister, Hazel."

Both girls favored their mother in personality and could chat up a storm. Toddler Hazel wasn't quite mastering full sentences, but she'd picked up several amusing phrases from her older sister.

"I'm Teagan." Green eyes dancing with delight, she bent from the waist and extended her hand to Annabelle. "Nice to meet you both."

The indulgent smile she bestowed on his nieces annoyed Chase. So did the way his gut contracted at the sucker punch of her flawless beauty and disruptive charm. He'd expected her to be high-strung and bossy, a showy woman who relied on her looks and superior attitude to take charge. Instead, Teagan was a disconcerting blend of sensuality and elegance.

Although Hazel was usually wary of strangers, she bloomed beneath Teagan's captivating smile and even reached out for a handshake. Before he realized what was happening, Chase caught himself appreciating the socialite's ease with the children. A second later, her eyes snagged his and their palms came together. The unrelenting sun and muggy air made her skin a bit sweaty and awakened the citrus notes in her perfume, making his head swim. Captivated by her beauty and charm, his body flared with sudden sexual awareness. Panic followed. How could he possibly find her attractive? Doing so was a keen betrayal of Ethan's friendship.

"Sawyer should be along any second." Hating the husky note in his voice, Chase loosened his grip, setting her free. He cast a desperate glance toward the street, willing Sawyer to appear and rescue him. "In the meantime I can fill you in on some of the house's background."

"You said we could have ice cream," Annabelle protested, tugging on his hand, the heat and her aborted nap making her cranky. "When are we going to get ice cream?"

"Ice cream," Hazel echoed, jumping up and down on his left.

"Soon," he soothed, glancing from the reproach in Annabelle's blue eyes to Hazel's flushed cheeks. He hit both girls with a winning smile, wondering if he could successfully tour the property before they melted down. "We just need to show Ms. Burns around this house."

"Why?"

The answer left a bitter taste in his mouth. "Because she might want to buy it."

Annabelle shot a dubious look at the place, taking in the weed-choked front yard and broken picket fence. "Why would she want to do that?" Her gaze shifted to Teagan. After taking her in, Annabelle leaned against Chase's leg and stage-whispered, "Is she crazy?"

Chase mustered all his willpower and just managed to keep from glancing Teagan's way. In somber tones, he declared, "It will be fixed up before she moves in."

"I don't know." Annabelle made no secret of her skepticism. "It's pretty ugly."

"Making ugly houses into pretty ones is what I do," he reminded her, flicking a look toward Teagan and finding her watching their exchange with interest.

"But this is really ugly."

"That's exactly why I want to buy it," Teagan put in, her gaze taking on a fervent glow as her attention shifted from Annabelle to the derelict house. "I'm excited to restore this house so that it looks beautiful like all the other homes on the block."

"We live in an old house," Annabelle announced, shaking her head. "My mom always complains that stuff doesn't work."

Teagan's lips curved in a wry smile. "Well, since your daddy is so good at fixing up old homes, maybe he could repair some of those things."

"My dad's a doctor." Annabelle beamed. "He fixes people."

"Oh." A line appeared between Teagan's perfect eyebrows. She shot a quizzical glance Chase's way. "I'm sorry. I thought…"

"He's not my daddy." This amused Annabelle to no end.

"I'm their uncle," Chase supplied as both his nieces dissolved into fits of giggles.

"I see…"

Teagan measured him with fresh perception, making Chase's temperature spike. Apparently, she approved of the view because a half smile appeared and invisible threads of enticement radiated from her, reaching for him. His heart thumped in hard, erratic pulses, flooding his system with adrenaline. This woman was even more trouble than Ethan had made her out to be.

"Yes…well…"

He was never at a loss for words, but his acute reaction to Teagan caught him off guard. Worse, somehow, he'd misplaced his integrity. Finding himself attracted to the woman who'd injured his best friend went against everything Chase stood for. Ethan had always counted on Chase to have his back, which wouldn't be the case as long as Chase perceived Teagan as anything other than a shallow, manipulative interloper out to harm anyone who got in her way. Time to dash icy water on this sizzling connection between them.

His phone pinged with a text. Glancing down, he scanned the message and ground his teeth. "Looks like Sawyer is delayed. She suggested we begin without her."

Teagan must've picked up on his irritation because she gave a crisp nod and reined in her sex appeal, becoming all business. "Of course. Let's get to it."

Teagan took refuge in business, needing a moment to catch her breath and let her swooning senses recover their equilibrium. Although Sawyer had talked up the talented renovation specialist, the single promotional shot of him on his company's website hadn't prepared her for the impact of meeting the handsome, powerfully masculine architect in the flesh.

And then they'd shaken hands.

As if the heavy Charleston air wasn't enough to raise her temperature, the sudden flash of heat when they'd touched had made a weird combination of goose bumps and perspiration erupt over her entire body. She was ridiculously glad that Chase Love was neither married nor the father of these adorable girls. While she'd met several charming men since coming to Charleston, not one had awakened a mad impulse to bat her eyelashes and swoon. The rugged renovation specialist inspired a giddy, breathless delight that made her want to melt against his sturdy, muscular frame.

Unfortunately, there was the little matter of the steely set of his jaw and flinty hazel eyes that took her in and found her wanting. Teagan would be blind not to see that the man didn't like her. Still, his broad shoulders and stern demeanor sparked a mischievous impulse to flirt with him. Not a great idea when Teagan wanted to be taken seriously as a real estate investor. Runaway hormones would be a major problem if she'd be working in close contact with Chase for the foreseeable future. *If* being the operative word.

She was in the midst of wondering how to convince him she was an earnest businesswoman with definitive goals when the younger of the two girls said something that inspired his lips to curve into a fond smile. Her heart did a somersault.

Holy…wow! From forbidding to dishy in the blink of an eye. Teagan found herself swooning all over again.

"Shall we start with the three smaller residences?" Chase asked, blessedly oblivious to her inner turmoil. "My sister should be along in fifteen minutes to pick up these two. It'll be better to see the main house without them as a distraction."

"Sure," she murmured, hoping he'd put down the heat in her cheeks to the unrelenting sunshine.

Chase gestured for her to precede him along the cracked concrete walk that led toward the lopsided front porch. Giving the main house a dubious glance, she headed past the crumbling Victorian and set her sights on the three buildings beyond. With Chase out of view, it was easier to reorient her thoughts and refocus on the reason she was here.

In addition to the main house, the large lot accommodated three guesthouses with individual addresses that she intended to fix up so they could become transition housing for women at risk. Teagan had been inspired to attempt the project after meeting Zoe Daily, owner of a boutique in downtown Charleston called Second Chance Treasures. The store specialized in arts and crafts items made by survivors of domestic abuse. Although she'd been looking for a historic home in need of renovation since coming to Charleston a month ago, Teagan was inspired to look for a property that could also serve women in need after hearing Zoe's story of living in the back room of the boutique after leaving her abusive husband while she financed her dream of helping other women in similar circumstances.

"Sawyer mentioned they were in better shape than the main house."

"They are. These houses have had tenants in them until recently," Chase said, keeping an eye on his nieces as they explored the overgrown backyard. "They were built in the mid-fifties."

A lockbox attached to the middle of the trio held the keys to all three. While Chase opened the front door, Teagan pursed her lips and pictured what she'd like to do to the exterior of each cottage. First of all, she intended to paint them bright colors to make each home feel special. White shutters and trim would tie them together.

Chase left to unlock the other two houses, leaving Teagan to peruse the middle one. A cozy living room, tiny kitchen, two decent sized bedrooms and a bathroom badly in need of updates. Lay down some durable flooring and add some modest but stylish furnishings and the place would be a sanctuary for women and children who badly needed a safe place to restart their lives.

"What do you think?" Chase asked as she exited the house.

"It's not as bad as I expected. Barring any hidden problems in the walls, I imagine I could have them fixed up and ready in a month." As Teagan checked out the other two houses, her enthusiasm for the project swelled.

"Ready to see the main house?" he asked, his expression less forbidding as he corralled his nieces and gestured toward the two-story Victorian.

"Sure."

The original paint color had long ago faded from the nineteenth-century siding. The decades of neglect left Teagan wondering how much of the home's original features remained intact. She was giddy with the idea of taking a historic home from disastrous to glorious. It would be so much better if the decorative moldings, heart pine floors and fireplaces were all there.

"Excuse me," Chase said before heading away from her down the front walk.

Teagan had been so absorbed in the house, imagining it painted a buttery-yellow with turquoise and soft coral accents, that she hadn't noticed a white SUV idling at the curb. A lovely blonde woman circled the vehicle to embrace the little girls. A sudden lump formed in Teagan's throat as mother and daughters reconnected. Not once growing up had she or Sienna been that joyful to see Anna Burns. Their mother had never been a warm, affectionate woman. Her demonstrations of love took the form of shopping sprees and elegant lunches where the girls were expected to behave like civilized adults.

A stab of resentment caught Teagan off guard. She didn't recall wanting her childhood to be different. Her adoptive parents Anna and Samuel Burns had given her everything money could buy and Teagan had no complaints about her private school education, designer everything or the incredible vacations in Europe. Sure, they didn't hug, nurture or read bedtime stories. That's what the nannies were for.

It wasn't until Teagan arrived in Charleston and was welcomed into the arms of her biological family that she discovered the joy of being loved. A year earlier she'd submitted her DNA to a genetic testing service in the hopes of finding her father or connecting with her mother's family. Never had she imagined that her search would lead her to Charleston.

Because her adoptive parents had raised her to be ambitious and prone to suspicion, Teagan had been on guard when her Southern family—her cousin Ethan excluded—had snatched her into their lives and showered her with gregarious affection. The lack of trust had led her to make a whole host of mistakes.

An overachiever from her crown to her toes, Teagan knew she couldn't leave Manhattan behind without having something to make relocating to Charleston worth her while. Running her biological family's company seemed like the perfect answer. That her cousin Ethan was already poised to become the next CEO of Watts Shipping was merely a hurdle to be cleared.

Unfortunately, her single-mindedness had led her to hurt the one person she'd always been able to rely on, her older sister Sienna. Adopted into the Burns family as an infant, Teagan's experiences growing up on the Upper East Side of New York City had taught her to battle fiercely to achieve her goals. The cutthroat world often favored circuitous methods instead of straightforward action. And she'd brought those tactics to Charleston with disastrous results.

Teagan hadn't taken into consideration that acting duplicitous wasn't in Sienna's nature when she'd badgered her sister into spying on Ethan for her. Nor had she predicted that her sister would fall in love with Ethan. It was Teagan's fault that the couple had gone through a disastrous breakup before reconciling. If Teagan hadn't been so focused on herself, she might've seen that something real and lasting had developed between the pair and backed off. Instead, she'd let stubborn determination blind her to what was best for Sienna.

Swept by uncomfortable emotion, Teagan turned her back on Chase and his family and concentrated on the house. The Victorian's flaws were something tangible she could repair and restore. So much easier than fixing the broken relationships with her sister and Charleston relatives. Those couldn't be improved by her design aesthetic or a bunch of money.

Since her biological family wasn't speaking to her at the moment, Teagan decided she'd demonstrate she wasn't a selfish, unfeeling shrew. She intended to behave. No more schemes or plots. She would display her philanthropic side by saving a historic home in downtown Charleston and offering three dwellings as a safe haven for victims of domestic abuse. In time, she hoped, someone would give her another chance.

"As you can see, the house is in rough shape," Chase stated as he joined Teagan in the home's gloomy twenty-foot-long foyer.

A zing of pleasure traveled along her nerve endings as his clean, masculine scent surrounded her like an enthusiastic hug. Her strong reaction to him was unexpected since he wasn't her type. Teagan liked her men charming and flirtatious. Chase Love was serious and principled.

Nor had she come to Charleston to find romance.

But that body. His beautiful face. And those piercing green eyes.

He was a tantalizing enigma and she couldn't bring herself to dismiss how he made her feel.

Tearing her gaze from his forbidding profile, Teagan glanced around her. Undaunted by the boarded-up windows, peeling wallpaper, water-stained ceiling and filthy pine floors, she surveyed the original fireplace details, nine-foot pocket door that separated the living and dining rooms and intact plaster details.

"I've looked at a lot of options around the downtown area," she said. "Some worse. Some in better shape. At least this one has a roof. And all the extra houses fit perfectly with my vision for the property."

"It's a lot to take on," Chase continued, shooting her a sideways glance.

"I don't know how much you know about my background in New York…" She strolled down the wide hallway leading toward the kitchen at the back of the house.

"Sawyer mentioned you've bought and rehabilitated several historic properties in Manhattan."

"I have. It's important to save architectural gems for future generations to appreciate."

Chase studied her for a moment before asking, "So, why not stay there and do that?"

Startled by his cool tone, Teagan's chin rose defensively. "Because I was hoping for a new start with my Charleston family."

Silence fell between them as room by room they moved through the house. Tiny tracks in the dirt indicated a whole slew of critters had invaded when the humans had moved out. Teagan's attention kept shifting between her surroundings and her heightened awareness of her muscular tour guide. His keen gaze missed none of the house's flaws and he took special care to point out every problem she'd encounter during the restoration.

"I feel as if you're trying to talk me out of buying the house," Teagan said as they stepped onto the sketchy front porch.

From their brief interaction, she'd gathered that he was a straight shooter, someone who wouldn't sugarcoat the situation or cheat her. Given the sketchy business practices she'd encountered in New York City and the incessant machinations of her social group, Teagan found Chase's candid approach refreshing.

"I just want to be clear." Chase grappled with the stubborn lock on the front door, before saying, "It needs a lot of work."

"I already knew that from the photos." Teagan couldn't stop smiling. Everything inside her was screaming that this was the property she was meant to have. "But most of the work will happen on the main house. It's really just cosmetic fixes for the three homes in the back."

"It's going to be expensive. And with a property this neglected, the potential for hidden problems is enormous."

"Regardless, I think this is the perfect project for

me." Unwilling to be deterred, Teagan stepped gingerly to the loose railing and surveyed the neighborhood. "I know I'm going to love it here when it's done."

Snorting at her enthusiastic proclamation, Chase deftly avoided the rotten boards as he descended to the safer footing of the front walk. While he waited for her to join him, Chase pulled out his phone and scanned the screen. During the tour, the smartphone had buzzed numerous times, but he'd never checked any of the messages. She was accustomed to managing multiple tasks at the same time, giving none of them her complete attention, but this man brought purpose and drive to whatever he set his mind to. Teagan found it both thrilling and daunting.

"I'm going to call Sawyer right now and put in an offer," Teagan said, pulling out her own device. She was in the process of scrolling through her contacts when Chase spoke.

"Before you do," he began in clipped, harsh tones, "you should know that I have reservations about taking you on as a client."

This was not at all what she wanted to hear. Still, she had sharp wits and charismatic charm in her bag of tricks.

"I see." Teagan set aside her frustration. She couldn't tackle a problem unless she knew what was wrong. "Anything you care to share with me?"

Chase pondered her question in silence, his features set into disgruntled lines. "Not yet."

As much as Chase's reluctance disappointed her, Teagan sensed it would do her no good to push him. "Thanks for meeting with me today. I'll let you know when I hear back from Sawyer that the buyer has accepted my offer."

They parted and headed to their cars. Before she got in, Teagan gave the weathered Victorian one long last look. In order to realize her vision for the property, Chase must accept her as a client. His passion for restoring historic homes matched her zeal for preservation. They would make a fantastic team and she intended to make him realize that. Because once she set her sights on something, she usually got it.

And right now, she wanted Chase Love.

Two

Without committing to any sort of follow-up meeting with Teagan Burns, Chase beat a hasty retreat. Earlier he'd scheduled a walk-through of a restoration project his company was handling. Now, as he met with the general contractor at the work site, he struggled to focus on the checklist of items he was concerned about. Instead, he found his thoughts returning over and over to the New York socialite. A glint of brass fixtures recalled how the sun turned her hair to liquid gold. The verdant garden behind the house summoned the mischievous sparkle in her eyes that had caused his chest to tighten.

Chase ground his teeth and cursed.

Banishing his acute reaction to her might've been possible if he'd encountered any problems at the construction site, but for once, the work was progressing smoothly. So, instead of chasing down missing materials or scrambling to reschedule trades, he had time and headspace to contemplate how he could've possibly been attracted to the woman.

Granted, she was gorgeous, the sort of elegant beauty that most men would appreciate and desire. But Charleston was filled with leggy blondes sporting come-hither smiles and none of them could compete with his passion for restoration—a fact that frustrated Ethan every time he tried to set Chase up.

Before meeting Sienna, Ethan had been one of the city's most sought after bachelors. He'd doggedly inflicted his packed social calendar on Chase, dragging him out to this function or that casual meetup. But Chase had little patience for small talk or meaningless flirting. The women he did make a connection with were ones in the market to remodel a home or redesign a space.

Yet when it came to Teagan, he'd struggled to keep his mind on the house tour. The distracting floral scent of her and the soft sounds of interest or approval she'd made had set fire to his libido. He knew a hundred details about the house, but he'd struggled to summon even the most basic of information. Thankfully, she'd been so wrapped up in taking the home in that she hadn't noticed his less than stellar performance.

Deciding he'd inflicted his ill humor on the crew long enough, Chase got back in his car and headed toward his office. He'd scarcely driven a few blocks when his phone lit up with a call from Sawyer. Based on his meeting with Teagan, he suspected Sawyer's news was about to complicate his life.

"I received a call from Teagan," she began after a quick greeting.

"And she wants to make an offer on the Calloway property," he declared, the lump of dread in his gut offset by an unsettling flutter in his chest.

Despite the New York socialite's commitment to bring the Calloway house back to its former splendor, the location of the home meant that she'd be his neighbor. Was that worth achieving his vision for the neighborhood?

"She thinks it's perfect," Sawyer continued, oblivious to his distress. "And she wants you to handle the renovations."

"I don't know that I have time," he hedged, even as the need to be involved bore down on him.

Sawyer huffed. "That excuse might work with other people," she said, "but not with me. I know exactly how important that house is to your family and how determined you are to see it restored properly."

"Yes…well…"

The situation surrounding this entire project was complicated for so many reasons. First was his mother's desire to purchase the property and their cousin's unwillingness to let her have it. Second, if Teagan bought the house and outbuildings, Chase's desire to manage the renovation would require him to work with her and that would surely rub Ethan the wrong way. Rock meet hard place.

"My mom's going to be disappointed that the house is going to an outsider."

"Maybe…"

Something in Sawyer's tone triggered his suspicion. "What are you not saying?"

"She might've already called me."

If Chase hadn't been driving, he would've squeezed his eyes shut in dismay. Instead, he hit his left turn signal and angled away from the office and headed toward his mother's house.

"What did you tell her about the house?"

"She already knew that Rufus put it on the market and asked me if you'd made an offer." Sawyer hesitated. "I told her about the call."

"Was she upset?"

"I'd say she's more determined than anything."

That sounded exactly like his mom. Chase wished for the thousandth time that Maybelle's personality had a little less steel and a touch more willow in it. Once her mind was set on something, she was hard to dissuade.

"I'd better go see her." And hopefully talk her into a more reasonable stance regarding the house.

"Good luck."

Chase headed south toward the 1843 home his mother had "downsized" into after her husband's death. At nearly five thousand square feet, with four bedrooms and five bathrooms, the house had been added on to several times over the years so that its original architectural style was hard to determine.

"Hello, Mother," Chase said as he entered the comfortable living room and spied Maybelle Love seated at her great-grandmother's writing desk. Crossing to her, he leaned down to kiss her cheek.

"What a nice surprise," she said, getting to her feet. Looping her hand around his left arm, she drew him toward the gold damask sofa near the big windows that overlooked the lush side yard. She sat down and patted the seat beside her.

He wasted no time. "Sawyer said you called her about the Calloway house."

Maybelle nodded. "I heard from my cousin Lemon that Rufus has put the house on the market again." Her blue-green eyes grew reproachful as she stared at her son. "How come you didn't call me about it?"

He steeled himself against his mother's disappointment. "I only just found out a few hours ago."

"And you couldn't take a minute to pick up the phone and keep me apprised of the situation?"

"I should have." Chase braced himself to explain to his mother that negotiations were dead in the water. Rufus had refused to even entertain their offer. "It's just that I wanted to have good news for you."

Relations had been strained between the two branches of Maybelle's family since the reading of her great-grandfather's will.

"Sawyer told me what happened," Maybelle explained. "I think we should definitely offer him more than what the house is worth."

"I'm not convinced there's a number high enough to overcome the bad blood between our families."

Maybelle waved her hand, dismissing Chase's concern. "Apparently, he's in dire need of an influx of cash…"

"That entire family is always in dire need," Chase grumbled, barely able to contain his exasperation with the whole messy situation. "He just won't sell it to us."

"Nevertheless, we should keep trying. You know how important that house is to me." The desperation in Maybelle's gaze tore at Chase's heart. "I couldn't bear it if someone ruined it."

"I won't let that happen," Chase assured her, determined to keep that promise.

His mother inhaled a ragged breath and stared out the window at the greenery beyond. She blinked rapidly several times, and then gave a pragmatic nod. "Then we'll have to figure out another way to save the house."

"Such as?" he questioned warily.

"Sawyer mentioned she has a client who is very interested in the property." Maybelle fixed her son with a sharp stare. "I understand you met with her earlier today."

Chase wasn't prepared to talk to his mother about Teagan's interest in the Calloway property when he hadn't yet decided if he should work with her. "She's an investor from New York."

He used the descriptor deliberately, knowing his mother wouldn't want the house to go to someone from "off," an outsider who couldn't fully appreciate the home's place in Charleston history.

"It's my understanding that she's quite passionate about restoration and intends to bring our historic property back to its former beauty."

His skin prickled as his mother's words sank in. Maybelle's enthusiasm struck him as odd. For decades he'd listened to his mother complain that her ancestral home was suffering from neglect and how she longed to purchase the property and save it for her grandchildren. Why all of a sudden was she so eager to let it go to a stranger?

"So she says." He kept his tone cautious.

His mother gave him a sharp look. "Do you have a reason to think she's not being up front with you about the house?"

The question caught Chase off guard. Maybelle should've heard that Teagan was on the outs with her Charleston family and the reason why.

"Nothing concrete," he admitted.

"What's she like?" Maybelle asked, her eyes bright with hopeful interest.

Chase pondered the myriad impressions Teagan had made on him, but decided against sharing those with his mother. The last thing he wanted to do was encourage her romantic notions. Ethan wasn't the only one frustrated with Chase's lackluster love life. Maybelle wanted both her children happily settled and disliked that each of them lacked a romantic partner.

Nor did he want to bring up Ethan's troubles with his long-lost cousin. So, that left Chase with sharing her professional background.

"She has some restoration experience," Chase said. "I understand she's done several projects in Manhattan."

"You know, if we can't buy the house ourselves, this might be a good solution. Sawyer said Teagan was quite impressed with the work you've done and would like you to head up the restoration." Maybelle beamed with maternal pride. "I know I would sleep better knowing the house was in your talented hands."

"Are you really at peace with having someone you don't know own your family's home?"

Maybelle clenched her hands together and turned somber eyes on her son. "If acquiring the property for us is impossible, we should make sure it falls into the right hands."

The Watts and Love families had enjoyed close social connections for decades. In fact, Maybelle and

Ethan's mother had been in the same debutante class; they'd married weeks apart and given birth within months of each other. Both families had hoped that Ethan's older brother Paul and Chase's older sister might be destined for each other. While that pairing didn't work out, Ethan and Chase had become fast friends while still in diapers.

"I understand what you're saying." The trouble was Chase didn't trust Teagan. "I'd really like to make Rufus another offer. Something he really can't refuse."

His mother emitted a delicate snort. "And what if he keeps us dangling and the house gets snapped up by someone else in the meantime?"

"The property has been empty and neglected for years. That's why thus far no one has been willing to pay what Rufus has been asking for it." Chase just needed a little time. "Let me try to find someone besides Teagan Burns to buy the property."

"Someone you can guarantee will want you to handle the restoration?"

Of course there were no guarantees. Waiting was a risk. For all any of them knew, a different buyer could demolish the house and build something brand-new. True, the value was in the land and the home's history, but not everyone shared Maybelle's passion for the latter.

"What exactly do you have against Teagan Burns buying the house?" Maybelle's gaze sharpened on her son. "Sawyer said she's passionate about historical restoration. Plus, she has the resources to do things right. It seems to me that she'd be your ideal client."

Hearing his mother echo Sawyer's earlier argument, Chase found himself stuck for an answer that would satisfy her without getting into the drama between her and Ethan.

"She's from New York and runs several businesses there. Eventually, she's going to have to head back. I'm concerned that once she's gone her interest in Charleston will wane. In all likelihood that will happen before the renovation is complete and who knows what will become of the property then?"

"Simple," his mother stated. "We'll buy it from her. In fact, this whole situation might be to our advantage. Rufus will never sell us the property, but we could cultivate an excellent relationship with Teagan Burns in the hopes that someday we can buy the house from her."

Unable to defend his persistent reluctance to have anything to do with Teagan or to refute his mother's clever strategy, Chase resigned himself to a long-term association with the New Yorker.

"That might work," he grumbled, anticipating a tense phone call with Ethan in the coming days.

"It will work." Maybelle looked satisfied for the first time since Chase had arrived. "And I think we should start getting to know Teagan right away. I want you to bring her by for lunch. You'll do that for me, won't you?"

"Of course." Chase recognized the futility of arguing with his mother, and could only hope that Teagan made a less than stellar impression. Because only then would Maybelle move heaven and earth to block the socialite from getting her family's ancestral home.

Immediately after touring the Calloway property, Teagan had called Sawyer Thurston and arranged to meet the real estate agent at Eli's Table in two hours for a cocktail. When she arrived, Teagan noticed the restaurant was next door to the Gibbes Museum of Art and wondered how many hours Sienna had spent pursuing the extensive collection.

Thinking of her adoptive sister cast a shadow over what had been a stellar day. Their estrangement nagged at Teagan, especially when she hadn't had any success persuading Sienna to respond to any of her calls or texts.

Apologizing didn't come easily to Teagan. From an early age she'd watched her parents navigate New York society. If people got in their way, sometimes they got hurt. The same lessons that taught Teagan to be ruthless aroused Sienna's sympathy. Teagan didn't enjoy the havoc she sometimes wrought, but she couldn't bring herself to let down her guard and show weakness either. Still, she'd been wrong to use Sienna the way she had. And admitting that out loud to her sister was the first step toward repairing their relationship.

If only Sienna would let her try.

While Teagan waited for Sawyer to arrive, she took several selfies and posted the best one on Instagram. Charleston provided her with an abundance of excellent photo opportunities to populate her social media account and by tagging all the various restaurants and shops in the area, she'd picked up a substantial number of new followers. The extra attention was nice, but she'd also noticed a drop in likes and comments from her New York friends.

It was a different world down here. Charleston was more like a weekend getaway for her Manhattan associates than somewhere they'd consider for a long-term move. And while they'd been enchanted by her early posts, as one week had stretched into several, they'd lost interest, preferring to gossip about weekend parties in the Hamptons, fashion and whatever flavor of the week struck their fancy.

Her phone rang. Although she didn't recognize the number, the area code was local. "Teagan Burns."

"This is Chase Love."

Her toes curled as his smoky voice filled her ear. "Chase." She almost purred his name. "Did you have a change of heart?"

"You might say that." He didn't sound particularly happy about it. "I have some architectural plans for the Calloway house at my office. You should come by and take a look at them. Then we can see if we're on the same page."

"I'd love that. But tell me…" His unexpected about-face had rendered her giddy. "Is this Charleston's version of inviting me up to look at your etchings?" In the silence that followed her words, she could imagine his dismay at her flirting.

"The plans are at my office." Once again, he'd met her banter with gruff practicality. "I don't know what your schedule looks like, but I have an hour at ten tomorrow morning if you are free."

Teagan rushed to accept the time, afraid he might change his mind about working with her. "Ten sounds perfect."

"Then I'll see you tomorrow."

Before she could say goodbye, he'd ended the call. Delighted by the turn in her fortune, Teagan began adding Chase into her contacts. She'd just finished capturing a screenshot of his profile picture from his website when a shadow blocked the afternoon sunshine. Assuming it was Sawyer, Teagan glanced up. The positive energy that had buoyed her since Chase's phone call died when she spotted the arrival.

"Declan."

She cursed herself for sounding like a breathless debutante but couldn't blame herself for the panic that flared. She'd never imagined her nemesis would still be in Charleston instead of eight hundred miles north in his corner office overlooking the Hudson River in Manhattan's financial district.

"Hello, Teagan."

Without asking for her permission, he settled on the chair beside her and crossed his long legs, his arm resting casually on the table to show off his Piaget Altiplano watch. Today's choice of exquisitely tailored suit was dove gray with a white shirt that he left open at the neck to reveal a triangle of masculine skin. Unable to recall the last time she'd seen him so casually turned out, Teagan applauded Charleston's heat and humidity for forcing him to surrender his usual sartorial elegance in favor of comfort. It was nearly impossible to get the better of Declan Scott.

Designer sunglasses hid his striking amber eyes, enhancing the air of mystery he loved to cultivate. While his opponents speculated about his next move, they weren't noticing that he was already five steps ahead of them. Heaven knew she'd learned that the hard way, too many times to count.

"You look as gorgeous as ever."

She wasn't fooled by his buttery tones. The man was a rattlesnake, poised to strike.

As a teenager, she'd been less immune to his swagger and the searing keenness of his soul-crushing gaze. That was before she understood the soul of an evil genius lurked behind all his dreamy masculine beauty. If he'd been in a movie, he would've been the villain intent on world domination. In the real world, Declan was a cagey businessman, determined to control the biggest share of Manhattan real estate and working toward that goal one ruthless negotiation at a time. The Brookfield Building stood in the way of his multi-billion-dollar development plans.

"Why are you still here?" she demanded, eager to get to the point of his visit.

"You are in possession of something I want."

"The Brookfield Building." The slim gold rings on Teagan's fingers glinted as she waved away his intentions. "I might sell it someday, but only to someone who will appreciate the beauty of its facade and the character it adds to NoMAD."

NoMAD, short for North of Madison Square Park, was an up-and-coming neighborhood once known for its cluster of wholesale stores along Broadway. Now, the area was anchored by a series of posh hotels and luxury condos. A high concentration of trendy bars and restaurants made it a popular spot for weekday after-work crowds.

The Brookfield Building had occupied the corner of 5th and 29th in Midtown Manhattan since 1895, withstanding the relentless march of developers determined to replace New York landmarks with sparkling glass monuments to their ambition and egos. Declan Scott was one of those developers. For the last five years he'd been busy buying up buildings that stood in the way of Scott Tower.

He'd battled preservationists anxious that Midtown could soon reach the tipping point between the architectural mix of old and new and watched in satisfaction as his opponents' applications to save historic buildings were rejected by the Landmark Preservation Commission.

Only the Brookfield Building remained as the last holdout. Until six months ago, the property had belonged to Edward Quinn. Despite pressure from Declan, he'd staunchly refused to release the architectural gem from his portfolio. The building held a special place in Edward's heart. It had been his first purchase, the foundation on which he'd built his empire.

Now Teagan owned it. "You're wasting your time. I'm not going to sell to you."

Unfortunately, no matter how many times she'd refused to sell it to him, Declan wouldn't take no for an answer.

Declan's vexation showed in the twitch of one eyebrow. "My latest offer will change your mind."

Teagan shook her head. It would not do to let him glimpse any weak spots in her defenses. "If Edward wanted you to have the building, he would've sold it to you before he died."

Or left it to his son, who didn't share his father's passion for historic buildings and would've agreed to sell the property to Declan before his father was even buried.

Instead, Edward had bequeathed the late nineteenth century ten-story building to Teagan.

She'd known Edward since childhood. The Burns and Quinn families had been neighbors in the Hamptons and it only made sense that when she wanted to know the ins and outs of Manhattan real estate, she'd interned at Quinn Real Estate.

Although he'd been both a mentor and a great friend, taking her under his wing and fueling her passion for preservation, Edward's decision to give her the Brookfield Building had been an enormous shock. To her. To Edward's family. And most definitely to Declan.

He'd been furious, even going so far as to accuse her of—how had he put it?—seducing the old man into leaving the building to her. The charge had proved that Declan Scott wasn't omniscient, but that didn't make him any less dangerous, as his latest stunt had demonstrated. He'd sent several anonymous texts to Ethan. By mixing inflammatory insinuations with a dash of truth, Declan had turned her cousin against her and almost destroyed Sienna's chance at a happily-ever-after with Ethan.

Declan inclined his head. "Why don't I buy you dinner and we can discuss it?"

"There's nothing to discuss," she pointed out in crisp dismissal.

She'd first locked horns with Declan in high school. She'd marched into Bennington-Hill Academy, a sophisticated freshman with her own jewelry line, confident in her ability to set trends and rule her classmates the same way she'd done at her former school. And of course, she had, but in the process, she'd challenged the status quo. Declan Scott had been very much at the top of the school's social hierarchy. He hadn't been interested in a tit-for-tat exchange; he'd nearly crushed her. Since then, they'd had numerous trifling skirmishes, but interfering in her attempt to establish herself in

Charleston went beyond anything either of them had ever done in the past fifteen years.

"Have you ever known me to give up without getting what I want?" Declan asked.

"I'll give you that. You are persistent." The increase in each successive offer demonstrated his determination to secure the land on which the Brookfield Building stood. "And you play dirty. Such as the anonymous texts you've been sending to Ethan. That was low. Even for you."

"You didn't give me much choice." A muscle jumped in his jaw. "If you'd just sold me the Brookfield Building, you would've never heard from me again."

"So, instead of accepting my decision, you decided to get personal."

"It's business," he shot back. "And I do whatever it takes to win."

"This isn't a seat on a charity board that will benefit me or a penthouse apartment I want to buy and renovate." She pointed a perfectly manicured finger at him. "It's my family. You and your tactics have caused irrevocable harm."

"That should give you a sense of just how important the property is to me." Declan leaned forward. "And you obviously needed to be reminded that I'm not the only one with something to lose."

Teagan kept her expression from revealing the deep anxiety she felt at this reminder. Already his interference had caused rifts with her family. She dreaded how much more he could do if she didn't give in. Ruthlessly she hardened her will and resolved to fight him no matter what.

Declan set a large white envelope emblazoned with

Scott Development's logo on the table. While she would never accept one of Declan's increasingly lucrative offers, wondering how much he intended to offer this time made her pulse accelerate. It wasn't that she needed the money or reveled in having something to hold over him—although watching him gnash his teeth at her series of refusals had caused several brief flutters of glee.

"The price is the same as before." He nudged the envelope in her direction.

She wasn't surprised that he hadn't increased his offer—he'd already bid double what the building was worth—but his confidence chilled her.

"I might not be able to match your experience negotiating deals," she said, "but I'm pretty sure you need to sweeten the offer once it's been turned down."

"You didn't let me finish." The left corner of his lips twitched as if he held all aces. "Sell me the property and I'll leave you alone."

Tired of his machinations, Teagan let her bitterness show. "I don't think there's anything left for you to ruin."

"There's always something more."

Her heart gave a big bump at the threat. "Edward didn't want you to tear down the Brookfield Building and entrusted me with it to make sure that didn't happen."

"Which only goes to show how his faculties had slipped in the last few years."

"Maybe." She shrugged off the double-edged insult. "But in the end, he still managed to beat you."

Although her comeback had surely drawn blood,

Declan was too skilled a negotiator to let that show. "I'm not beaten."

No. And she could see from the way a muscle jumped in his jaw that he intended to fight on until the bitter, bloody end. She just hoped she was still standing when the dust settled.

Three

"Let me see if I understand what's going on." Ethan's scowling face filled Chase's computer screen.

Chase's best friend was calling from Savannah where he was currently spending time working at his biological mother's company, trying to decide if he wanted to succeed her as CEO or continue to work for Watts Shipping and eventually end up running his adoptive family's company.

Like Teagan, Ethan had also utilized a genetic testing service to search for his biological relatives. Around the same time as she'd been discovering her Charleston roots, Ethan had connected with his birth mother, Carolina Gates. Chase knew that as happy as this had made his friend, the discovery had produced a complicated mix of emotions in those around him.

"Teagan wants to buy that rundown relic your mother

has been trying to get her hands on for years," Ethan continued, "and you are considering helping her renovate it?"

"Rufus won't sell the property to us," Chase pointed out, splitting his attention between his friend's tirade and the budget figures for an extensive renovation project that was close to completion. Thanks to several unexpected issues, he had to figure out a couple places to cut expenses and then convince his client they couldn't afford to spend a hundred and twenty-five dollars a square foot for tile. "If Teagan gets it, she's committed to doing a historic restoration rather than tearing it down or turning it into a modernized nightmare."

"What makes you think she'd be willing to let you take charge of the restoration?"

"We spoke." Chase's thoughts shot back to that meeting and his unwelcome attraction. "She's coming by in an hour to view the drawings I did for the house and look at the old photos of the place."

Given how much of the house's plasterwork had been lost to neglect, he was fortunate to have so much original reference material to work from. Since his mother had been trying to buy the house for years, Chase had a file filled with copies of original blueprints, historic photos and his own architectural renderings of how they could bring the house up-to-date while preserving its authentic charm. This wasn't the first time Rufus had entertained selling the house he'd let fall into neglect since his grandmother Francis had died ten years earlier. Chase was quite convinced that his third cousin enjoyed tormenting Maybelle by opening up the possibility that he would let her have the house only to snatch the hope away.

"Have you lost your mind?" Ethan demanded. "Why would you even consider letting her get her hands on your family's property?"

Bristling at his friend's unfair charge, Chase shifted his full attention to the computer screen. From the moment Sawyer had put Teagan together with the Calloway property, Chase had known he would be torn between his loyalty to his mother and his best friend. Their diverging goals and opinions meant he couldn't please both.

"This house is important to my mom," Chase stated, his tone crisp and determined. "I will do whatever it takes to save it. And Teagan says she's committed to a restoration."

Ethan must've noticed he'd pushed his friend too far because his tone became more reasonable. "You can't trust her to do the right thing."

"I understand your skepticism." Chase sighed. "But Teagan could be our only shot at influencing what becomes of it."

"Okay. Let me think about this." Ethan's eyes narrowed in a way that Chase recognized and had learned to dread. "Maybe this can work to our advantage."

Chase dug his fingertips into the tense muscles at the nape of his neck and braced himself. "How so?"

Oblivious to his best friend's disquiet, Ethan laid out his plan. "By handling this restoration, you are in the perfect position to keep an eye on her while I'm away in Savannah."

Ethan's proposal was the exact sort of thing Chase had been dreading.

"There's no one else I can count on to do this."

"What about Poppy or Dallas?" Chase suggested,

listing Ethan's twin cousins. "I'm sure they'd be happy to keep an eye on her."

"Although they're mad at her now, she's likely to get them back on her side."

After meeting the delectable New Yorker, Chase couldn't argue. Even though Teagan's scheming to usurp Ethan's presumptive role as future CEO had led to the alienation of her sister, as well as all her cousins and two sets of aunts and uncles, she wouldn't rest until she'd redeemed herself in their eyes. Plus, she had her grandfather in her corner. Grady Watts was so thrilled to have his long-lost granddaughter back in the family bosom that he'd turned a blind eye to her underhanded ways.

"You, on the other hand," Ethan continued, "are the one person she won't be able to charm into getting her way."

Normally, Chase preferred substance over style, but the way his meeting with the enticing Teagan Burns had gone, he might not be as invulnerable as Ethan believed. Still, he kept that bit of disturbing data to himself and offered up an alternative excuse.

"Look," he said, "this isn't a good time. I've got a dozen projects in various stages of completion and the nominations for the Carolopolis Awards are due by the end of next month. I don't have any free time to spend with your cousin."

"She's dangerous," Ethan argued. "I don't want anyone else to get hurt. Hey, you know I wouldn't ask if it wasn't absolutely necessary for me to spend time in Savannah with my mom and figure out what I'm going to do about her job offer."

Biting back a curse, Chase nodded. "I get it. I'm just

not sure what you expect me to do with Teagan. It's not like I can follow her around Watts Shipping or anything."

"I'm not really worried about Watts Shipping," Ethan said. "I clued Dad into what Teagan's been up to on that front and it's not like he's going to hand over the reins to someone with no experience. I'm more concerned about what might happen with the rest of my family. If Teagan was willing to use her own sister to get what she wanted, imagine what she would do to the relatives she barely knows."

"I don't know why you're worried." Chase pictured the three women Ethan had mentioned. "Those three can take care of themselves."

"Humor me."

Chase should point out that Ethan could turn to his adoptive brother for help, but the cybersecurity expert was newly engaged to Lia Marsh and determined to avoid any of Ethan's future machinations.

Many months earlier when their grandfather Grady had grown ill and lost his will to live, Ethan had come up with an insane ruse to introduce a stranger as Grady's long-lost granddaughter so he could meet his beloved daughter's child before he died. The ploy had unexpected results. Connecting with his granddaughter caused Grady to rally. He stepped back from death's door and regained his strength. Unfortunately, this left Ethan, his brother Paul and the counterfeit granddaughter, Lia Marsh, embroiled in a complicated mess.

By the time the truth came out, Lia and Paul had fallen in love and not long afterward the genetic testing service had connected the family with Teagan.

"So?" Ethan prompted. "Will you help me out?"

Despite his distaste for the task, he and Ethan were as close as brothers and Chase would do everything in his power to keep Ethan's family safe. "Fine."

"I knew you would." Ethan beamed at him. "Thanks."

After grumbling something in response to his friend's warm appreciation, the call ended and Chase turned his attention back to the overstretched budget. Half an hour later he had the numbers back under control and had emailed the client his notes on the changes they would have to make. Which left him with five minutes to prepare for Teagan's arrival. Not enough time for him to collect his wits and decide on a plan for how to balance Ethan's request against his own moral compass.

Chase unrolled the architectural plans for the Calloway property and weighed down the four corners with glass paperweights featuring photos of his two nieces. As his gaze traced the exterior lines of the main house, he pondered what it would mean to his mother to see the property restored to its former glory.

Promptly at ten, Teagan appeared in his office wearing a long floral skirt and a white sleeveless crop top. For several erratic heartbeats he stared at her in tongue-tied appreciation while she crossed the room with her hand extended. A standard business handshake sent ripples of awareness across his skin and he was beset by the urge to yank her closer so he could slide his lips along her neck.

Chase wasn't given to poetic imagery, but caught himself comparing the scent of her to sun-kissed magnolias and succulent peaches. It wasn't that she smelled like either of those things, but both evoked pleasant memories and reminded him of a time when he'd been happy.

"Wow, when did you have time to pull all this together?" Teagan's verdant gaze took in the table covered in drawings, giving Chase a much-needed moment to recover.

He cleared his throat, struggling to shake her effect on him. "I've worked on architectural drawings for the Calloway property for a long time."

"And all these photos of the inside?" She picked up one of the family photos and studied it. "Did you get these from the former owners?"

"Some of them. I've been collecting reference images for a while."

She circled the table, taking everything in while he strove to keep his attention off the expanse of bare midriff between the hem of her top and her skirt's waistband. This proved impossible. One glimpse of her toned abs left him adrift in the desire to coast his fingertips over her pale skin.

"Do you do this much extensive research with every home you restore?"

"Not every one." Chase ground his teeth and wrenched his complete focus back to the blueprints. "This house in particular is one I am quite familiar with."

"Because?" She raised her eyebrows and waited for his answer. When he took too long to respond to her prompt, she prodded, "Oh, come on. You opened the door."

"It doesn't matter."

"Now I'm intrigued." She sidled closer. "But I think you knew that I would be, didn't you?"

Her bare forearm brushed his, short-circuiting his judgment. "The house belongs—" Chase stopped himself just in time and resolved to keep quiet about his personal connection to the job until he decided if he should accept the project. "—to an old and prominent family."

"That's all fascinating. With all the historic homes you restore, I'll bet you've heard dozens of stories about Charleston's oldest families. I'd love to hear more."

Seeing the avid interest on her beautiful face, Chase pumped the brakes on his storytelling. With his promise to Ethan hanging over him, Chase opted for self-preservation. "I don't think that's a good idea."

"You have to eat, don't you?" From the look of Teagan's winning smile, she wasn't going to give up easily.

"I'm very busy and…" It wasn't like him to beat around the bush. He had many reasons to keep things between them strictly professional, but top of the list was his acute attraction to her. "Before we agree to work together on this project, I need to set you straight on something."

Taking in his grim expression, Teagan inclined her chin with slow deliberation. "Such as?"

While he recognized that what he had to say next might just cost him the chance to restore his mother's ancestral home, Ethan's favor chafed Chase's conscience like forty-grit sandpaper.

"Ethan is my best friend."

Although her brows knit and her lips tightened, Teagan's voice reflected curiosity rather than irritation as she asked, "And that's important because?"

"When he found out you were interested in buying the Calloway property, he asked me to keep an eye on you." Chase paused to gauge her reaction to his announcement. "In case you planned to make more trouble for his family."

Well...hell.

As Teagan absorbed Chase's words, her guard automatically went up at this revelation. Disappointment, humiliation and annoyance tumbled through her. Well, at least she now understood his grim, unfriendly vibes. How disappointing that the first man she'd found attractive in a long, long time was predestined to dislike her.

"I'm not sure what Ethan told you—"

A lifetime of self-preservation had given her strong defenses. No matter how badly she was hurt, she'd never let anyone know that she gave a damn one way or another. Yet, for some reason she did care how this man perceived her.

"You used your sister as a pawn in a bid to become the next CEO of Watts Shipping."

While her first impulse was always to defend her tactics as sound strategy, in this case, the scheme had hurt Sienna and damaged their relationship. She'd behaved badly and intended to fix what she'd broken.

"And I regret it."

"Do you? Or are you just telling me what you think I want to hear?"

A thrilling little shiver stole up her spine at Chase's merciless stare. Teagan sucked in a long, slow breath to calm her madly erratic pulse. When had it ever excited her to be scolded after being caught red-handed in one of her schemes? Never. She far preferred when everyone feared her. Among her fellow socialites, she'd never cared if people disliked her and took it for granted that everyone gossiped behind her back.

She appreciated the way Chase put his opinion of her on the table and wasn't daunted by his obvious dislike. Knowing exactly where she stood with him was a refreshing change. And her sense that no amount of flirting or charm would change his attitude provided an intriguing challenge.

"How about I tell you my side so you have a better understanding of me?"

He crossed his massive arms over his broad chest and nodded. "I'm listening."

Since coming to Charleston and meeting her birth relatives for the first time, she'd discovered that family could be warm and loving rather than distant and critical. Yet she hadn't fully appreciated the way they'd enthusiastically embraced her, and had continued to employ the sort of maneuvering that was second nature to her in New York. Her win-at-any-cost attitude had caused her to bully her sister Sienna into a scheme aimed at beating out her cousin Ethan for the top spot at their family's company. Her tactics might have been devious, but her motivation was straightforward.

"My adoptive family owns a property development company in New York City," she began, wondering if her story would encourage Chase to sympathize with her motivation. "And I'd always hoped that one day my father would decide to put me in charge instead of my older brother."

Chase stood silent and still beside her, a powerful presence that gave her the support she needed to keep going. It wasn't that she believed he would accept any explanation she might make. Chase was Ethan's friend, and as such, he was on her cousin's side. But she longed to tell her side of the story, bare the whole ugly truth, and maybe by owning up to it, she might be forgiven.

"But you see my father is…old-fashioned." Hearing the stress in her voice, Teagan paused and closed her eyes briefly to suppress her anxiety. "He intended my brother Aiden to take over Burns Properties."

"You think you should've been in charge?"

"Father made it very clear that I wasn't in the running. No matter my qualifications, ambition or strong work ethic, I was not his biological child."

Teagan hesitated to explain further. Exposing her vulnerabilities only ever led to her getting hurt. She'd gone as far as she could outside her comfort zone.

"Is that why you started looking for your biological family?"

"In part."

How could she begin to explain all the years she'd hungered to be with a family who truly wanted her? How she'd ached for the mother that had died when she was less than a year old? Wondered if her biological father knew she existed. Growing up she'd hated how being adopted made her an easy target for her classmates and the way her adoptive mother showed her off like a custom-made gown.

Meeting her Charleston relatives had filled the gaping hole in Teagan's identity. She was the granddaughter of Grady and Delilah Watts and the niece of firstborn Miles—currently at the helm of Watts Shipping—and eldest daughter Lenora, who had married well and produced twin daughters Poppy and Dallas with husband Wiley Shaw. And she was the daughter of Ava, youngest of the three siblings. Headstrong and free-spirited, Ava had fled the family fold, running away to New York at the age of eighteen with the intention of becoming a world-famous model and instead ending up pregnant.

Before coming to Charleston, Teagan hadn't known that when Ava had left South Carolina, she'd cut all ties, so her family hadn't known about Teagan or the fact that she'd been barely a year old when Ava had died in a tragic accident.

"Look," she continued, "everything I told you, it's not an excuse for my motivation or how I handled things. Just because Ethan was adopted and I was biologically a Watts didn't mean I should get to run the company."

His clear hazel eyes bore into her. "If you wanted the CEO position, you should've worked hard and beaten Ethan fair and square."

Teagan acknowledged his point with a nod. "Let's just say that in my experience, working hard isn't always enough for me to get what I want."

"So you manipulate situations to get what you want."

"When I have to." She didn't like his disappointed expression and vowed to change his mind about her. "It's always served me in the past, but things haven't worked out for me here. In less than a month I've manage to alienate my entire Charleston family. Poppy and Dallas barely speak to me. My aunts and uncles are coolly polite. The only person who doesn't seem at all bothered is Grandpa Grady and I think that's because he has no idea that I was the reason Ethan and Sienna broke up."

"So, why don't you go back to New York? Sawyer

mentioned that you own several profitable businesses there."

Teagan's heart melted. Chase would have no idea how gratifying it was to have her successes recognized as opposed to her failures.

"I'm stubborn," she replied. "When I want something, I make sure I get it."

"And you want to be the future CEO of Watts Shipping."

Teagan shook her head. "I don't belong there. It was just my ego that made me go after the job in the first place."

"Then what's here for you?"

"My family." A tight ball of misery formed in her gut as she contemplated all the missteps she'd made since coming to Charleston. Initially, she'd been too arrogant to recognize that she was an outsider here and behaved like an entitled brat. She was determined to repair all that she'd damaged, but wasn't sure if any of them would forgive her. "And the opportunity to make my mark on Charleston."

"By renovating a historic property."

"And contributing to the community by providing transitional housing for women in need," Teagan put in, reminding him of her altruistic leanings.

"You're still maneuvering so things work out in your favor," he pointed out with relentless disapproval.

"Clearly my scheming ways are a part of who I am and difficult to shake," Teagan began, shifting her attention to the drawings of the three houses on the back of the property. "But I'm not the horrible person everybody believes me to be. I really do want to help people."

To her relief, a flicker of uncertainty clouded Chase's features. Maybe she was finally getting through to him. Good.

"Given what happened between Ethan and me, I can see why you hesitated to be involved in this project at all. What changed your mind?"

"What makes you think I have?"

His aggressive tone caught Teagan off guard. She'd touched a nerve and this wasn't a man to toy with. Still, her curiosity couldn't be contained.

"Given all the time and energy you put into planning this renovation, I can't imagine that you'd be happy to see someone else taking over the project." Impulsively, Teagan let her earlier attraction shine bright as she grinned at him. "And I think once you get to know me, you'll discover I'll be a fantastic partner."

From the moment she'd turned around the day they met and had spied him approaching her, she'd been bowled over by his masculine energy and vigorous good looks. But what had slipped past her defenses had been his sweetness with the little girls.

Her initial assumption that he was their father had compelled her to tamp down the fierce and overwhelming rush of attraction. The fever that had seized her in those first moments was unlike anything she'd ever known. Struck by a hunger to give herself to him and drown in his pale green eyes, her entire body had been consumed by a sizzling energy.

Even now, knowing that he'd been set on her by Ethan, Teagan couldn't set aside her baser instincts and behave sensibly. This man lit a fire in her blood and she wanted to revel in the heat.

"Would you be free for lunch?" With her family giving her the cold shoulder and Sienna not speaking to her, Teagan was feeling isolated and more than a little lonely. "To discuss the project further," she elaborated, finding herself oddly breathless. "I'm sure you'll see I'm one-hundred-percent committed to doing the best, most accurate historical restoration of this property. We'll be a great team. Just wait and see."

While that was true, she also craved more time in his company. The fond way he'd smiled at his nieces told her that a warm heart lingered beneath his gruff exterior. Add to that her physical attraction to him. How every time their gazes collided, butterflies exploded in her stomach. Still waters ran deep and she couldn't wait to discover what else lay beneath his impenetrable exterior.

"I'm afraid I don't have time today."

That wasn't a definite no and Teagan decided to capitalize on it. "How about tomorrow then?" she coaxed, eager to spend more time with this perplexing man. "My treat."

"It's really not necessary."

She cocked her head and regarded him. "Are you playing hard to get?"

"No, not at all," he retorted, sounding shocked. "It's just that this is our busiest time of the year with the nomination deadline for the Carolopolis Awards fast approaching."

"Well, you have to eat sometime. How about dinner?"

"Dinner?" The way he echoed her invitation with a dumbfounded expression did little to bolster her ego.

"You're supposed to be keeping an eye on me, right?" She had no idea what impish compulsion had prompted her to hurl that revelation back at him. "What better way than to join me for dinner?"

"You won't let up until I accept, will you?"

"See, you get me." Feeling as if she'd won an important skirmish and not wishing to rub it in, she regarded him solemnly. "We're going to work well together."

He snorted. "If by 'well' you mean you'll badger me until you get your way."

His observation delighted her. "You're not like Ethan, are you?"

"How so?"

"He's a better schemer than you."

"That's never been up for debate. Be it business or personal, I have always found that situations are less complicated if I'm up-front."

"Maybe I should give that a try."

"Based on how things have been going for you with your family, it might be a good idea."

Teagan couldn't help herself; she laughed. "You don't pull any punches, do you?"

"Not when I think someone can handle it."

To her dismay, she found her cheeks heating beneath the frank directness of his gaze. "And you think I can?" She wasn't sure if he'd offered her a compliment or criticism.

"I'm certain there's little you can't handle."

Again, based on his matter-of-fact tone, she wasn't sure whether to take his remark as praise or reproach. He was Ethan's best friend and destined to take her cousin's side. Yet, she warmed to his words as if he liked her strong personality.

"Mostly that's true, but I get the feeling you're more than a match for me."

This seemed to catch him off guard. "Why do you say that?"

"Because I'm not accustomed to people who call me out and it's rather refreshing."

"Really? I would think you'd hate to get caught scheming."

"Not really. Where I come from, if you're not the one manipulating the situation, you're the one being outmaneuvered."

"It won't do you any good to try to control me."

"No," she mused, curiously excited by his challenge. "I don't imagine it will."

Chase scrutinized her for several seconds before nodding. "I'll pick you at seven o'clock tomorrow night."

Teagan beamed. "I'll be counting the hours."

Four

"You told her I asked you to keep an eye on her?" Ethan's voice blasted through the phone speaker.

As soon as his meeting with Teagan had ended, Chase had called Ethan to share how things had gone. "Yes."

"Why would you do that? Now she knows we're on to her."

"She already knew that." Chase employed the overly patient voice he used when his nieces were particularly tired and irritable. "And you know I'm not one to play games. Plus, it should deter her from acting out if she thinks I'm keeping an eye on her."

"You don't know Teagan. She's relentless." Ethan's exasperation gave way to a huge, resigned sigh. "Well, since we don't really have a choice, let's try it your way."

Chase refrained from pointing out that they were already doing it his way. "Good."

"Between you and Paul, I have too many straight shooters in my life."

"You're welcome," Chase said, familiar with his best friend's grumbling.

Ethan's older brother was a former police officer who currently owned a cybersecurity business and shared Chase's tendency to see the world in shades of black and white, good and bad, right and wrong. Both Paul and Chase had pursued martial arts as kids and Chase's hero worship of Ethan's older brother had always bugged him, especially during a phase in high school where Chase had considered pursuing a career in law enforcement. But in the end, it was construction that captured his imagination and heart. After college he took over East Bay Construction, the company his family began twenty years ago, and partnered with Knox to double the size of the business.

"So, what's your plan for keeping an eye on Teagan now that she's on to you?"

"We're having dinner tomorrow night."

"Dinner?" Ethan sounded dumbfounded. "You asked her out to dinner?"

"No. She asked me. She wants to discuss my ideas for the Calloway property."

"Be careful."

"It's dinner." Hearing his friend's doubtful grunt, Chase added, "Strictly professional."

"Since when do you date your clients?"

"Since my best friend asked me to keep an eye on his cousin. How exactly did you think I was going to go about that?"

"I thought maybe you'd be more discreet."

"Like maybe I'd skulk around Charleston, peering at her from behind bushes?"

"Sure. That works."

"You know, if you're unhappy with my methods, you can always find someone else to do your dirty work."

"There's no one I trust."

That wasn't completely the case, but Chase decided against mentioning Ethan's brother Paul in this particular moment. "You don't sound as if you trust me."

"It's not you I'm worried about."

Chase was reflecting on his last conversation with Ethan as he stopped his SUV outside the Birch-Watts Estate. Picking up Teagan at her grandfather's house came uncomfortably close to this being a date. Part of him was tempted to sit in the car and honk the horn to let her know he'd arrived, but his mother would skin him alive if she heard he'd done something like that. Instead, heaving a gigantic sigh, he exited the vehicle and trudged up the curving stairs to the front door.

Chase had spent a considerable amount of time here growing up. The extensive grounds included a pool and had been a frequent gathering spot for friends and family. The Federal-style house had been built in 1804 and remodeled several times, but always with an eye toward preserving and enhancing its original architecture. Although he'd never been involved in any of the updates to the main house, Chase had remodeled the carriage house several years earlier and turned it into a cozy living space.

Grady's housekeeper ushered Chase into the spacious foyer and indicated the formal living room. Chase had arrived a few minutes early and hadn't expected

Teagan would be ready. In fact, he expected that she'd keep him waiting. To Chase's delight, the living room wasn't empty. Grady sat near one of the windows, his cane beside him, a recently released biography in his hands.

Knowing how concerned the family had been by their eighty-five-year-old patriarch's failing health, it was good to see Grady looking so robust. The return of his long-lost granddaughter had given him a reason to live. Chase just hoped Teagan didn't disappoint him.

"Good evening, Grady," Chase said as he settled into a nearby chair.

Grady looked up from his book and smiled. "Chase. Good to see you. What brings you by?"

"I'm here to pick up Teagan. We're having dinner."

The old man's eyebrows rose and his eyes danced with pleasure. "You don't say. Well, you have good taste. My granddaughter is both beautiful and accomplished. I think you two will make a fine couple."

Before Chase could correct Grady's misinterpretation of the situation, a feminine voice spoke from the doorway.

"Oh, Grandpa don't scare him away." Teagan shot Chase a saucy wink as she went past him and settled beside her grandfather. She slipped her arm through his and dropped a quick kiss on Grady's cheek. "If Chase thinks I have designs on him, he'll play hard to get."

"Why would he do that?" Grady asked, taking Teagan's hand and giving it a quick squeeze. "He'd be lucky to have you."

"That's sweet of you to say." Her voice quavered slightly as if Teagan was gripped by some overpowering emotion.

The affection between Teagan and her grandfather looked real, but Chase recalled her saying that Grady was the only member of her family who was speaking to her at the moment. Perhaps she was playing at being a doting granddaughter to preserve this final relationship.

"You be good to my girl." Grady fixed Chase with a stern glare. "She's having a rough time at the moment."

Chase opened his mouth to point out she'd been the one who'd caused the trouble to begin with but ended up nodding instead. "Of course. She's in good hands." Why he'd added the second part, Chase had no idea.

Grady looked satisfied. Teagan glowed with smug delight.

"We'd better get going." Teagan deposited another kiss on his wrinkled cheek and then stood. "I'll see you tomorrow morning for breakfast."

"Have fun, you two."

After bidding Grady goodbye, Chase followed Teagan to the front door. Once they were outside and out of earshot, he shot her a dark look.

"What was that all about?"

"Whatever do you mean?" she asked, all innocence and sweetness.

"You gave Grady the impression that we're dating."

"I thought it sounded better than explaining that Ethan asked you to keep an eye on me in case I feel like getting up to more mischief."

Before meeting up with Teagan tonight, he'd been perfectly comfortable in his lightweight blazer. Now, as he watched her glide down the steps ahead of him, each stride flawless in her impossibly high heels, Chase found his temperature rising. Another woman exhibiting her outrageous behavior would've left him cold. But every scorching glance, the tantalizing body language that beckoned to him, her provocative quips all made his temperature spike.

Tonight she wore a shimmering gold minidress that screamed sophisticated New Yorker. With her long blond hair braided and pinned in a loose updo with face-framing wisps, she was glamorous, ultra-feminine and brimming with confidence. Conflicting emotions consumed him. For all she drove him crazy, his desire for her remained constant and compelling.

"You could've explained that it was a business dinner," he pointed out, opening the passenger door for her.

She slipped into the vehicle. The move caused her hem to rise and Chase was helpless to resist stealing an appreciative glance at her long, toned legs.

"I could've. But then I wouldn't have had the chance to watch you stew."

Before he could take the bait, Chase closed the door and circled to the driver's side. As he slid behind the wheel, he asked, "Have you told him you made an offer on the Calloway house?"

"I did and I explained that you and I are going to work together to restore it." She paused while he started the engine and put the car into gear. "Grady told me your mother's cousin refused to sell her the property after he inherited it."

While this wasn't common knowledge in the community, the Love and Watts families had a long history of friendship. Grady would think nothing of sharing the information with Teagan. Chase had opened the door by mentioning that the property was important to his mother and then refused to elaborate. For a schemer like Teagan, ferreting out these sorts of secrets would be second nature.

"Why is that?" Her avid gaze acted like a truth spell on him.

"There's bad blood between our families going back for generations."

Might as well tell her the whole story and deny her the satisfaction of dragging it out of him. Not that denying her gave him any pleasure. The ludicrous notion ricocheted around his brain, making his head hurt. How had this woman gotten under his skin so fast, compelling him to consider what she would and wouldn't enjoy?

"It must've been something terrible for your families to still not be getting along."

He'd told her more than he intended to—might as well spill all of his family's ugly past. "My great-great-grandfather split his fortune between his two children. The daughter inherited money while the son inherited the business and the house. She invested well in her husband's business and her family thrived. He lacked her sound judgment and ran the family business deep into debt." When he paused to consider how much more to share, Teagan's rapt expression prodded him to continue. "Rufus has the same terrible business sense as his father, grandfather and great-grandfather and resents how well my mother's side of the family has done for themselves. I don't think there's any amount we could offer him to overcome his bitterness."

"This must be terribly hard on your mother."

Chase steeled himself against Teagan's sympathy. If the woman wasn't twisting his hormones into knots with her flirting, she was tricking his emotions with her clever insight.

"She's very sentimental."

"And you're very protective of her."

Even though his mother had a backbone of Southern steel, he'd always done his best to cushion the blow each time Rufus turned down their purchase offers.

"She's my mother."

The restaurant he'd chosen was a five-minute drive from Grady's house and he was lucky to score a nearby parking spot.

"You know," Teagan began, as he shut off the car and jumped out before she could finish her thought.

Chase opened the passenger door for her and Teagan shot him a warm smile as she exited the vehicle. "The restaurant is this way."

As they strode side by side toward the restaurant, she finished her earlier thought as if no time had elapsed. "It's really sweet the way you worry about your family. And it's not just them, is it? I'll bet you safeguard anyone who's important to you."

She spoke as if this was something exceptional. Wasn't protecting loved ones just the right thing to do?

"Can we please just focus on the Calloway restoration tonight?"

"Oh, we'll get to that." An intriguing smile bloomed on her pale pink lips, stirring his discomfort. "But first, I want to learn everything there is to know about you."

So she could figure out how better to manipulate

him? Chase growled in irritation. "There's not much to tell."

"You underestimate my interest." Teagan raised an eyebrow while her eyes danced with beguiling amusement.

Rumbling with displeasure, Chase opened the restaurant's front door and ushered Teagan into Fig. The establishment's clean, simple decor was the perfect backdrop for its excellent culinary offerings. Since they sourced locally, the menu changed with the seasons and Chase visited frequently.

The hostess led them to a linen-clad table against the wall. While Teagan settled onto the booth seat that would give her a view of the restaurant, Chase settled opposite her, facing the blank white wall which provided nothing to distract him from her beautiful face.

A waiter appeared to welcome them and get their drink order started. Teagan pursed her lips as she studied the menu.

"I feel like something bubbly to celebrate our first date," she said. "How about a bottle of the Ruppert-Leroy champagne?"

While the waiter nodded his approval, Chase sighed. Would it do any good to protest that they weren't on a date? Teagan was a force of nature when she set her mind on something. And while Chase was not a pushover, he decided to save his energy for the important battles ahead.

Once the champagne had been served, Teagan lifted her glass and toasted, "To the beginning of a successful partnership."

Chase echoed her salute, deciding this was a pledge he could get behind. Despite being polar opposites in temperament and behavior, Chase believed they were of like minds when it came to the restoration of the Calloway house. It was because of this, and to ensure his mother's peace of mind, that Chase was willing to put up with Teagan's provocations.

"So," Teagan began, her eyes dancing with mischief. "What is it you do when you're not making Charleston beautiful?"

"Eat and sleep." It wasn't far off, but he didn't want to bare his personal life to Teagan. Seeing her determined expression, he added, "Since I have a tendency to take on too many projects, I work all the time."

"How did you get into renovation?"

"My mother is passionate about Charleston," he explained. "Its history, architecture, culture. She's active in the Preservation Society and sits on the boards of several local museums."

"That tells me a lot about your mother, but little about you. When did you know you wanted to be an architect?"

"After my dad died. I was a sophomore in high school at the time." Refusing to be drawn into a moment of connection, Chase glanced away from the sympathy reflected in Teagan's expression. "My mom took over running East Bay Construction and I started helping out with the renovations after school and during my summer breaks. I think both Mom and I felt close to him doing the work he loved."

"I'm sorry for your loss. That had to be a tough age to lose your dad." She made a little face. "I don't know why I said that. There's no easy age to lose a parent."

As he nodded in agreement, it occurred to Chase that Teagan had never had time with either of her birth parents growing up. She'd come to Charleston in search of her mother's family. He wondered if she'd had luck locating her father.

"My mom died before I turned one," Teagan continued, her mood contemplative. "I'm sure it was devastating to lose her, but I don't remember that time or her at all."

"What about your dad? Did you have any luck finding him through the genetic testing service?"

"No." A flicker of something caught his attention before she veiled her gaze with her long lashes. "But I did learn who he was. Unfortunately, it wasn't until after he died. He sent me a letter through his lawyer."

The vagueness of her explanation roused Chase's curiosity, but he was reluctant to probe. He'd never seen her this subdued, and this deeply contemplative side of her engaged his protective instincts. Beneath her sassy, confident exterior lay a tender spirit that had seen its share of sorrow. The urge to throw his arm around her and nestle her into the shelter of his body thrummed in him.

"So, he knew who you were."

She gave a rough little laugh. "All along, apparently. He was more than twice my mom's age, with a family." Her lips tightened as if she was fighting emotion. When she spoke again, her voice shook. "I don't know if it was one night or a torrid affair. The one clear fact is that I was a big mistake."

"Did he say that in the letter?"

"No." She shook her head and her melancholy scattered like droplets of water. "But he wasn't in a position to divorce his wife and abandon his kids so I'm sure my mother's pregnancy wasn't exactly welcome news."

"So you have half brothers and sisters?"

"One of each."

Chase wondered if she'd reached out to them. "Are they in New York?"

"Yes."

"Did you contact them?"

"He asked me not to."

This struck Chase as unfair.

"At first it bothered me." A pregnant pause hinted at how much. "But in the end, it's what motivated me to contact the genetic testing service and here I am."

And to Chase's surprise, he was glad of it. Despite the troubling drama she'd brought to all their lives, her keen interest in saving the Calloway house made her the perfect partner for him.

"Wait." Her eyes narrowed. "How come I asked you a question and ended up being the one baring my soul?"

"Obviously, you needed to get it off your chest and share it with someone."

"I did." She sipped her wine and stared contemplatively at the candle on the table between them. "No one else knows about my real dad."

"Not even your sister?"

Teagan gave an awkward half shrug. "I was crushed that he wanted me to keep our association a secret. It made me feel unwanted and you've probably figured out that I'm not accustomed to letting down my guard. Sharing something that painful…" She trailed off with a grimace.

Then why are you telling me?

Even as the question popped into his head, Chase was hammered by a startling development. He'd become her confidant. The role made him uncomfortable.

It implied an intimacy that went beyond client/contractor. He wanted a professional relationship with her. She was a complicated, vexing woman who somehow managed to stir his protective nature as well as his libido.

Keeping his distance was imperative. But every time he tried to resist, she drew him in. How else could he explain why he'd agreed to have dinner with her? Or why he noticed the nuances of her body language and expressions?

"Okay," she gusted out on a breathy laugh. "Enough about me. I know you don't work 24/7 so what is it you do for fun?"

"Martial arts." When Teagan's eyes widened, he added, "I'm a black belt."

"You don't seem the type." She cocked her head and scrutinized him. "I mean, you're built like someone who could kick ass, but you don't strike me as… aggressive."

Chase heaved a resigned sigh and gave her his standard answer. "Consistent training not only conditions the mind and body to have strength and stamina, but also helps the body fight disease, stay flexible and strong. It also provides stress relief and releases pent-up energy."

Her lips rounded into a surprised *oh*. "Sounds like I should give it a try."

This was not what he'd expected her to say, but since she'd given him an opening, Chase had a suggestion. "I teach a beginner's class on Wednesday afternoons. You're welcome to come."

Teagan nodded enthusiastically at his invitation. "Just tell me where and when and I'll be there."

He'd thrown the suggestion out there never imagining she'd agree so readily. Should he warn her what to expect? That would be the right thing to do. But Teagan enjoyed teasing him too much and he deserved a little payback.

"We can have dinner afterwards." His offer erupted before he had a chance to consider what he was thinking.

Teagan blinked in surprise, and then grinned in delight. "I'd like that."

At the studio where Chase trained and taught, Teagan stepped out of the locker room wearing borrowed martial arts gear, the long white belt tied in a tasteful bow at her waist. Initially at a loss for what she was supposed to do with the thick material, she was feeling pretty smug at her artful styling. While she knew her New York friends would ridicule her for wearing the shapeless pants and jacket, something about donning the required ensemble made her feel physically powerful.

Flipping her long blond hair over her shoulder, Teagan strode toward the studio where the classes were being held. Before she reached the end of the hall, however, Chase stepped out of an office and caught sight of her. To her dismay, a shiver raced across her skin as she took in his solid frame dressed in all black. He pivoted in her direction, his pale green eyes taking in her appearance. A disgruntled scowl pinched his brow.

"That's not how you wear the belt."

"No?" Uncharacteristically giddy beneath his raking regard, she peered up at him from beneath her lashes, all too aware that any attempt at flirtation would fail, but compelled to try anyway. "You'll have to show me. I've never done this before."

With a grunt of acknowledgment, he snagged one end of the bow and tugged it loose. The abrupt move pulled her toward him. Pulse racing, she held still as he unceremoniously gathered the belt into his hands, and then wrapped it around her waist twice. He had to put his arms around her to complete the move and with mere inches separating them, she inhaled the rain-kissed scent of his shampoo. No overpowering after-shave or cologne for this man, just the fresh scent of soap and the invigorating mint of toothpaste.

Damn.

Her mouth watered. She wanted to devour him, to slide her lips over his smooth, tan skin and nibble her way along his throat. Her hands were clutching his sleeves before the impulse registered. Still in the process of tying the belt, he started to step back and noticed her grip. One eyebrow arched.

"Sorry." With effort, she straightened her fingers and released him. "I…" Unable to summon an excuse, she shook her head.

With brisk, efficient movements, Chase stuck his fingers between the belt fabric and her stomach, pulling one of the loose ends through the space he made. Teagan clenched her teeth and bit back a groan at the contact. There was nothing personal in his touch, but that didn't prevent her nerve endings from going on full alert. It was growing clear that her physical attraction to this man would be her downfall.

"There."

Lost in her body's agitation, she'd missed that he'd

completed his task. Glancing down at the perfect knot, she murmured, "Thanks."

"Let's go."

He might not like her, but Chase was a Southern gentleman through and through. Turning aside, he gestured for her to precede him into the studio. Teagan took an unsteady step forward and then another, the fog clearing from her brain as she erased the proximity between them. She was almost breathing normally as the studio occupants came into view.

Teagan stopped dead as her gaze landed on her fellow classmates. After surveying the five- and six-year-olds dressed in their all-white *dobok* uniforms, she glanced over her shoulder at Chase.

"You neglected to mention that it's a beginner's class for *children*."

"Did I?"

She could swear a hint of amusement crept into his flat response, but his expression remained bland. Still, she was convinced that he'd deliberately set out to throw her off-balance. Well, he'd succeeded.

Before she'd come to Charleston, a stunt like this would've provoked her swift and vicious counterattack. Her keen defenses, honed through growing up as an adopted child to movers and shakers on Manhattan's Upper East Side, never permitted her to look foolish or anything other than in complete and seamless control. New York's exclusive social scene was a dangerous place for the gullible and inattentive. The sweet and kind were ripe for ridicule and destruction. Strike the first blow or die an excruciating public demise. Being on top was the only place to be, but the battle to stay there was never-ending. Someone was always trying to cut her legs out from under her. Like a spy behind enemy lines, she was constantly watching her back.

Unfortunately, she'd brought this edgy, paranoid energy with her to Charleston. Too late to avoid damaging her reputation with them, she'd recognized that her biological relatives were genuinely delighted to receive her into their family. She didn't need to scheme or manipulate anyone to gain position or acceptance. If she'd only trusted their warm welcome and explored joining the family's shipping company instead of acting like an entitled jerk and deciding it was her right to run the company, maybe she wouldn't be on the outs with everyone now.

She'd never loved being viewed as the villain, but appreciated the power it accorded. Her enemies, acquaintances and even some of her friends in New York were afraid to cross her. But since coming to Charleston and being wholeheartedly embraced by her true family, Teagan had noted a change in her attitude. At first the shift had been subtle and too weak to combat a lifetime of conditioning, but after her huge blowout with Sienna had sent shockwaves rippling through her Charleston family, Teagan had recognized that she'd messed up all her relationships.

A lifetime of conditioning left her struggling to break through her guards. It tore at her to have failed so badly with the family that meant so much to her. How did she make it right when everyone turned their back on her?

Calling upon the breathing techniques she utilized in yoga class, Teagan strode to the back of the group and offered a tight smile to the little girls on either side of her. They seemed to find their adult classmate acceptable because after casting welcoming grins her way, they sobered and focused on the tall man at the head of the class.

Without saying a word Chase captured the attention of every student. His commanding presence radiated authority and the rambunctious group settled, awaiting instruction.

Chase began by snapping his feet together, slapping his palms on the outside of his thighs and bending sharply at the waist. All the children imitated him.

"Today we're going to be working on three things." He paused briefly. "Repeat after me. Yes, I can."

The whole group chorused the three-word declaration. In an instant the energy in the room went from zero to ten, but Teagan found herself a beat behind. Determined to do better, she was focused and on the ball when the children showed off their biceps and repeated, "Do my best!"

"And finally," Chase said. "Discipline."

Teagan didn't think she was feeling paranoid when Chase's gaze touched on her as he spoke the word. No doubt he thought she could use some.

Teagan found herself captivated as well, but for a slightly different reason than the children around her. Her social group was filled with powerful men: billionaire businessmen, trust fund darlings with the world at their feet, European royalty and even a few professional athletes. Yet for all their money, success and charm, none of them awakened the hunger that filled her as she watched Chase guide his young charges.

By five minutes in, Teagan's heart rate was elevated, not only by the sight of Chase but by the physical exercise, and she wondered if she could keep up. She was feeling a little less overwhelmed when Chase sat them all down for stretching. Thanks to yoga, her flexibility was stellar.

After class, Teagan made a beeline toward the bathroom to freshen up and change back into the white lace cropped pants and matching off-the-shoulder top. She slipped her feet into hot-pink sandals, returned the borrowed *dobok* before making her way to the lobby. Since Chase had not yet arrived, she fluffed her hair and quickly uploaded the selfie she'd taken in the *dobok*. She'd picked up a bunch of new followers in recent days who were gobbling up everything she posted about her Charleston visit. No doubt they would be intrigued that she'd taken up martial arts.

"Are you ready?"

Chase had appeared while she was checking on the latest posts from the clothing line she ran with her mother. Since coming to Charleston, she'd turned over the social media for the company to her assistant and was pleased to see how well Angela was handling the account.

Teagan slipped her phone into her clutch and smiled at him. "Of course."

Chase pushed open the studio door and gestured for her to precede him. "The restaurant is nearby." He frowned as he regarded her four-inch heels. "Are you okay to walk there?"

"I live in New York City."

"So, is that a yes?"

"I regularly walk several miles a day in shoes just like these," Teagan explained with a wry smile. "So, that's a yes."

His response was a terse nod. "We're going this way."

"You're really good with the kids," Teagan remarked as they walked side by side down King Street. Her heart fluttered and thumped with each casual brush of his arm against hers. She couldn't remember the last time she'd felt this giddy in a man's company. It didn't help that Chase Love was tall, virile and adorably stern. "They hung on your every word and move."

"You sound surprised."

"I guess I am." How could she phrase this without stepping wrong? "You're so...big and...intimidating."

Yet everyone seemed to see straight past his unsmiling demeanor to the devoted heart that motivated him.

"I only intimidate the people that cross me."

His words made her shiver. Goose bumps sprang from a keen yearning to never get on his bad side. She didn't fear him physically. Despite his size and martial arts training he would never do harm. She knew that. No, the real danger lay in his negative opinion. Given that he'd heard nothing but terrible things about her, what chance did she have to win him over?

Their destination turned out to be The Darling Oyster Bar. Tucked into a historic hundred-year-old storefront, the airy restaurant's predominantly white decor was broken up by brick accents and pops of color in the form of mint green booths.

"I should've asked if you like seafood," Chase said as they waited for the hostess to return.

"I love it," Teagan answered, surveying the cozy space.

It was then that she realized every female in the vicinity had noticed him. The reason was clear. The man truly was a work of art. His face was all classic masculine angles with chiseled cheekbones and a jawline that could slice open a girl's heart. The perfection of his muscular form combined with his absolute confidence ensured that Chase was sucking up all the oxygen in the room.

Teagan stepped a little closer to him to assert her claim and scowled at the smiling hostess who'd greeted Chase by name.

"It'll be an hour for a table," she said.

"Popular spot," Teagan murmured, delighted the delay would enable her to spend more time in Chase's company.

"How long for the raw bar?" Chase asked.

The hostess glanced toward the horseshoe-shaped bar beside the front windows where customers sampled from the restaurant's wide selection. "We have two seats open now."

Chase turned to Teagan. "Are you ready to taste some of the best oysters around?" His eyebrows rose as if challenging her to refuse. "Or we can wait for a table."

Teagan had never backed down from a dare. "Bring them on."

Approval flashed in his eyes, warming Teagan to her toes. Her hunger for him to like her was off the charts. The realization caught her off guard. She'd stopped looking to others to validate her around grade school. What was it about Chase that made her crave his admiration and respect? The man had done nothing but cast skeptical glances her way and display no sign of recognizing her abundant appeal.

What she wouldn't give to have him overcome by

desire. To back her against a wall and seize her mouth with his. She'd clutch his powerful shoulders and encourage him to glide his long-fingered hands over her every curve. Teagan grew a little short of breath just imagining their tongues coming together in the perfect mating dance.

"Are you okay?" Chase's matter-of-fact tone banished her erotic daydreams.

Teagan blinked and found him peering down at her. Somehow, while she'd been caught up in her thoughts of him, they'd been seated at the raw bar. Off-balance and sizzling with unsettling cravings, Teagan let herself go along with the flow. She was usually too guarded to act impulsively. But something about Chase encouraged her to set aside her need to control the outcome and let her emotions lead her.

A lock of his dark blond hair had fallen over his forehead and obscured his eyes. Before she could second-guess the wisdom of reaching out to him, she'd brushed the thick strands to one side.

"You need a haircut."

He reared back as if she'd struck him and Teagan felt her cheeks heat. Blushing? Impossible. Losing her cool wasn't something she did.

"I'll make an appointment with Poppy," he murmured, avoiding her gaze.

At the mention of her hairstylist cousin, Teagan took herself in hand. This wasn't a date. He was spending time with her to keep her from doing damage to her family. The reality of the situation struck her like a lash.

"She's really talented." Embarrassment poked at Teagan. Why couldn't she stop herself from acting like an idiot around Chase? What had happened to her slick New York sophistication? "In fact," she continued, sliding her hand beneath the heavy curtain of her waist-length hair. "I was thinking about turning her loose on my hair. The heat down here makes me want to get rid of this length. Maybe I'll try a lob."

"Lob?" Chase echoed.

"Long bob. About here." Palms down, Teagan rested her fingertips on her shoulder to demonstrate the length.

To her immense shock, Chase reached out and pinched a strand between his fingers, testing the texture. "Your hair is nice as it is."

Electricity raced from her scalp to her toes, but it was his compliment that rocked her. So, of course, instead of graciously accepting the praise, she blurted out the first glib thing that came to her mind.

"Wow," she croaked. "I think that's the first nice thing you've said to me."

"That's not true," he countered, releasing her hair and turning his attention to the menu. "I remarked on your form during class."

Struggling to recapture her wits, she murmured, "You did approve of my stances."

She had no idea why teasing the serious man entertained her. Maybe it was his immunity to her light-hearted flirting. To her surprise, bright color appeared high on his cheekbones. Was he blushing? Maybe he wasn't made of stone. His nieces had certainly brought out his softer side. The fond smiles he'd sent their way had sure aroused a disconcerting flutter in her heart.

"You caught on quickly." Chase ordered a neat Monkey Shoulder scotch and Teagan echoed his choice. "I wish all my students paid such good attention to my instruction."

"Well, your students are five-year-olds, so I think the bar is pretty low."

He shot her a searching look that Teagan leaned into. Tingling awareness zinged through her. His muscular shoulder was mere inches away, Teagan's heart bucked. A myriad of sensations besieged her senses, all of them deliriously fun and intriguingly dangerous. She couldn't stop her gaze from running along the imperfect line of his nose that looked like it might've been broken a time or two. Nor could she steady the erratic pace of her heart as she let her senses open to him. She wanted to burrow her fingers into his thick hair and absorb the heat of his skin.

"Shall we start with Single Ladies?" Chase asked, yanking her focus back to the restaurant.

"Single ladies?" she repeated dumbly, convinced she'd missed the context of his question.

"Would you rather try something else?"

"Um…" Rarely did she get caught completely flat-footed. "No, I mean, I guess that's fine."

"They're my favorite. I think you'll enjoy them as well."

"Huh." She sipped at the whiskey the waitress had set before her and regarded him over the rim of the glass.

"What?"

"I didn't get the idea that you were such a ladies' man."

Chase frowned at her. "I'm not."

"Then what's with all the talk about single ladies?"

He pointed to a line on the menu. "We are here to eat oysters, right?"

"Oh." Teagan focused on the writing and mused. "So, *those* are the single ladies you like to eat."

"You really are a troublemaker, aren't you?"

Teagan offered up a cheeky smirk. "It's all part of my charm."

Five

He absolutely, positively could not, should not, find Teagan Burns attractive. She played games, manipulated people for her own gain and thrived on making him uncomfortable. If another woman exhibited any of these behaviors, he'd have walked away. However, because of these exact stunts, he'd committed to keeping an eye on Teagan, which meant he was also around for those brief unguarded moments that revealed other facets of her personality. The wry humor. Self-doubt. And the most tantalizing and hardest for him to resist, her passion for historic buildings.

Rather than notice the cool floral notes of her perfume or the delicate bones where her upper arms and shoulder came together, Chase focused his attention on the crisp Chablis he'd ordered to pair with the delicious raw oysters the server placed before them.

"Is there anything else you need?" she asked, her attentive gaze darting between Chase and Teagan.

Teagan surveyed the platter containing a dozen locally sourced oysters and shook her head. "This looks perfect." She picked up her wine glass and held it toward him. "To my first Charleston oysters. I'm glad to be sharing them with you."

Too steeped in Southern manners to leave her hanging, Chase lifted his glass and tapped it to hers. The delicate chime was nearly lost amidst the chatter of voices in the high-ceilinged space, but somehow the tiny sound resonated like a crash of thunder in Chase's chest.

"I hope you find them to your liking."

"Oh, I'm sure I will. After all, good company often elevates one's enjoyment of a meal, wouldn't you agree?"

Had she heard the husky undertones that roughened his voice? Her teeth flashed in a quick smile as he sipped his wine and watched her over the rim. Convinced her dancing green eyes were casting a spell on him, he resolved to work harder to keep his guard up in her presence.

"Flirting with me will do you no good," he declared, gesturing for her to choose the first oyster.

"That's where you're wrong." Teagan selected an oyster and dotted it with cocktail sauce. She brought the shell to her mouth, but instead of slurping it straight down, she inhaled the scent of the oyster. "You've underestimated the amount of pleasure I get from seeing you fight to keep from enjoying yourself when I do."

"You couldn't be more wrong about me."

"Really?"

Teagan loosened the oyster with the tiny fork and

placed the shell's edge against her lips. Chase sat mesmerized as the oyster disappeared. He watched her jaw work as she chewed and caught himself leaning forward in anticipation of her next words.

"Then I guess your reactions are all part of my imagination," she purred, settling the oyster shell face down on the bed of ice. "And you're not the least bit intrigued by me."

The sudden, warm pressure of her fingers against his thigh made Chase jump. All too aware that his involuntary reaction had proved her point, he sucked in a frustrated breath between his teeth.

Chase placed his hand over hers, determined to pull her fingers away, but found himself unable to do so. "Oh, I'm intrigued."

"Good."

She sounded far too smug for his liking. Acting in a way that was completely foreign to him, Chase cupped the side of her face with his free hand and leaned over to plant a strong kiss on her smiling lips. Her body froze as he grazed his teeth over her lower lip and flicked his tongue forward to taste her. The sweet tang of cocktail sauce blended with the fruity Chablis, and he groaned softly as she leaned into the kiss.

A chorus in four-part harmony blasted joyously through his brain as he savored the contact with her soft mouth. Fierce pleasure shook him to his core. Chase was a heartbeat away from losing himself in the white-hot joy when he remembered where they were. Setting her free took all his willpower. With his equilibrium battered by his loss of control, Chase returned to his former position.

"What was that for?" Teagan asked, a raw note of confusion in her voice.

"You weren't angling for a kiss?"

"Maybe." Hot color bloomed in her cheeks. "I don't know."

Chase let a raised eyebrow do the talking for him.

"Fine, yes!" Her half smile took the sting out of her aggrieved tone. "Since when does a proper Southern gentleman kiss a lady in a crowded restaurant?" She raised her hand. "And don't tell me I'm not a lady. Or claim you're not a proper Southern gentleman. You know what I mean."

"I guess you bring out the worst in me," he said.

"Funny," she mused, her eyes softening to rain-drenched willow. "I think you could bring out the best in me."

Chase had no idea how to respond so he turned his attention to the platter of oysters between them. "What did you think of your first Single Lady?" he asked, selecting an oyster. He loosened it with his fork before tipping the shell and letting the oyster slide into his mouth.

Teagan watched him with rapt interest. "You don't use any of the horseradish or cocktail sauce."

"The better to taste the oyster."

She followed his example on her second one and made a delicious sound, half moan, half murmur of agreement. Chase caught himself wishing they were somewhere private so he could take their earlier kiss further. He resisted the urge to dig the heels of his hands into his eyes and wipe away the image of them naked and writhing against each other.

What was wrong with him? Was he really thinking about sleeping with Teagan? The ache in his body was impossible to ignore. He wanted her more than he remembered wanting any other woman. The shock of it frustrated him. He needed to keep his head in this game. He owed it to Ethan and his mother to make sure his interaction with Teagan didn't blow up in their faces.

Even though he had no idea what exactly could go wrong, he knew becoming physically involved with her would put stress on their working relationship. And how could he explain to Ethan that he'd fallen under her spell?

"Thank you for bringing me here," Teagan said.

"There are a lot of restaurants in Charleston that serve outstanding seafood dishes."

"I'd love to visit a few of your favorites with you." She slid him a hopeful look.

A warning bell sounded, but as Chase spent more and more time in her company, he found the alarm easier to mute. "I think we can make that happen."

Her eyes flared as if she hadn't expected him to agree. A second later, she seemed to give the matter more thought. "This is lovely and you're being an exceptional escort, but I do have to ask if the only reason you invited me is because of the favor you're doing for Ethan."

He knew what she was getting at. With the chemistry between them taking on a life of its own over the last week, she'd shared a lot about her background and life in New York. Bottom line, she was far more complex and sensitive than she showed the world. As to whether this would lead him to trust her, Chase had yet to figure out.

"I did make a promise," he said, ducking the answer she wanted.

"And that's all there is to it?" Teagan's intent gaze probed his expression, digging for reassurance.

"No."

His grudging answer prompted relief to flicker across her expression. The momentary vulnerability disappeared so fast he wondered if he'd imagined it.

"I'm very attracted to you," she murmured, "and I want us to get to know each other better, but I wouldn't want to make the mistake of getting between you and Ethan."

The idea that he would have to choose between her and Ethan hadn't occurred to him until this moment. Nor did he think the decision would be all cut-and-dried. The more time he spent with Teagan, the more fascinated he became. Who knew what would happen after a long renovation?

"If you behave yourself," he reminded her, "there won't be any problems."

At his words a wicked smile curved her luscious lips. "What fun is it to behave myself?"

Chase breathed a sigh of relief at her quicksilver return to flirting. She was bossy and sure-footed when it came to manipulating the people around her. Serious, reflective Teagan was dangerous to his self-preservation. "Maybe if you avoid meddling with your family, we could avoid future disagreements."

"But then you wouldn't be tasked to keep an eye on me." Her palm made contact with his thigh once more. "And I think you like what's happening between us."

Her touch was just as unsettling this time around. In fact, he was finding it difficult to concentrate on anything except his thundering pulse. With the urge to kiss her growing too sharp to ignore, he set his fingers beneath her chin and coaxed her upper body closer.

"It pains me to say this." He brushed her lips with his. Excitement sparked at the glancing touch and he savored the sweet pain. "But you might be right."

Dressed in pastel workout gear, Teagan stood on the screened second-floor back terrace of her grandfather's mansion and listened to the sounds of feminine voices coming from the pool behind the house. Several times a week her cousins joined Ethan's future sister-in-law Lia in the morning for an hour of paddleboard yoga. Prior to falling out with her cousins, she'd often joined the trio and basked in the easy camaraderie. But once her relationship with her biological family cooled, Teagan had felt unwelcome and stopped going.

It wasn't like her to retreat after a setback, but she'd had such optimism about becoming part of the Watts family. Unfortunately, her New York style of getting what she wanted didn't work in Charleston. Instead of fitting in, she'd become a pariah.

And it wasn't just her Charleston family she'd upset. The one person she'd always believed she could rely on had cut ties. Sienna hadn't deserved to become Teagan's unwilling pawn. Reflecting on every decision she'd made since coming to Charleston, Teagan recognized that a lifetime of never quite feeling as if she fit in had driven her to act badly.

She'd never allowed any of her New York friends to glimpse the insecurity that fueled her behavior. All too aware that her adoptive mother only valued her beauty and that she had no worth to her adoptive father at all, she grew up determined the world would recognize her intelligence and ambition.

Squaring her shoulders, Teagan made her way down the outside stairs to the path that led through the dense foliage of the estate's lush garden. Anxiety made her stomach churn. Teagan had made mistakes before and suffered the consequences, but she'd always brushed criticism aside. This time it was different. These people were her blood relations and she couldn't treat the rift lightly.

She shouldn't have been surprised when upon spying her coming toward them both Poppy and Dallas abandoned their yoga positions and paddled toward the pool's edge.

"Good morning," Teagan said, failing to keep the disappointment out of her tone as the twins exited the pool. "I guess I'm too late for morning yoga."

"I have to get to the salon." Poppy tossed her sister a speaking glance while wrapping a colorful sarong around her slim form. "Catch you later." She directed the remark to no one in particular, but Teagan was sure it didn't include her.

"And I have menus to finish up for tomorrow's dinner party at the Harrisons'." Dallas picked up her board and followed her sister toward the two-bedroom carriage house they shared on the estate.

During the flurry of the Shaw twins' exit, Lia had sat cross-legged on her board, a tranquil lotus floating on the turquoise pool. Now, she shot Teagan a searching look.

"I guess they still hate me," Teagan remarked, sitting on a chair by the side of the pool.

"They don't hate you," Lia corrected, getting to her

feet and assuming the warrior pose. "It's just that this family is tight and very protective of each other."

Once again Teagan faced a painful truth. For all that she was a Watts by blood, she remained an outsider. "I get that and I don't really blame them for keeping their distance. I screwed up trying to mess with Ethan's future at Watts Shipping."

"Unlike most everyone else, I don't think you're solely to blame for what happened. When Ethan started getting those anonymous texts warning him about what you and Sienna might be up to, he could've discussed them with you instead of letting the whole thing become one big pointless game."

Preoccupied with her own mistakes, Teagan had never considered that Ethan had played a part in the whole debacle. "Why didn't he ask me about the texts?"

"Because he thrives on intrigue in much the same way you do."

Teagan winced. "I wouldn't say I thrive on intrigue. More like it's how I learned to cope with difficult situations. All too often I found that talent and hard work wouldn't get me what I want. So, I found alternative ways to achieve my goals."

Her social circle didn't include intimate friends. Her adoptive parents and brother weren't the emotional sort and their approval came after she'd succeeded at something. Growing up she'd equated acceptance with achievement. Receiving positive reinforcement for doing whatever it took to win had given her a skewed notion of best practices.

Her Charleston family was different. They'd welcomed her with open arms and no expectations. She hadn't had to prove her worth to them. They'd accepted her as she was. Unfortunately, rather than embracing the supportive environment, Teagan had fallen on old habits.

"So, I've been thinking of a way to fix things with the family and to prove that I'm more than what they've seen so far. Before I came to Charleston, I'd decided to make a positive contribution to the city. I'm hoping to create transitional housing shelters for victims of domestic abuse as well as fund programs that will offer these women career training."

"That all sounds amazing. And since Dallas is getting closer to opening her restaurant, she would benefit from your business expertise."

"I'd really love to help her with that." Teagan grew more optimistic. "Any idea how to reach Poppy?"

"I think what would go furthest with her is if you reunited with your sister."

"Sure. Of course." But even as Teagan agreed, she wondered how to repair the breach in her and Sienna's relationship. "I've already reached out to her many times, but she's not quite ready to talk."

"Sounds like you two just need to get into the same room."

"With her and Ethan living in Savannah at the moment, that's even less likely to happen."

"Maybe you need some help."

"What kind of help?"

"Rumor has it you've been out with Chase Love a few times. Why don't you ask him to reach out to Ethan for you?"

"I don't know," Teagan said, cringing as she imagined proposing Lia's idea to him. "Chase is pretty anti-scheming."

"Even for a good cause?"

"Even so."

Lia looked thoughtful for a moment and then nodded. "Well, I'm sure something else will occur to you. In the meantime, just keep coming down for morning yoga and making an effort. I'm sure they'll see that you're trying."

Following Lia's advice, Teagan reached out to her sister once more as she walked back to her bedroom. She wasn't optimistic that Sienna would answer, and wasn't surprised when she'd received no response in the time it took her to shower, dress and head to her favorite coffee shop.

Since it was Saturday and she had no plans for the day, Teagan took a detour on her way back to Grady's house. It had been not quite a week since she'd put in an offer on the Calloway house and she grew more anxious to hear back from the seller with each hour that passed.

She didn't need to get into the house; the memory of the tall ceilings and beautiful original fixtures were embedded in her mind. Instead, she wandered past the main house and into the back courtyard where an old wrought iron bench had been left to rust. She sat and gazed around the overgrown landscaping, imagining the azaleas trimmed, flower beds bursting with vibrant plants and the brick walkways restored. With a fountain offering trickling music, the space would become a soothing sanctuary for women who had not known much peace, and a playground for their young children.

Her thoughts turned to the man who would bring her vision to life.

Chase Love continued to confound her. And damn, if that didn't make him more fascinating. His kiss—

kisses—had done thrilling things to her insides. And when he'd admitted to wanting her, she'd nearly dragged him from the restaurant and around the corner to the nearest boutique hotel. Not that she could've manhandled him if he didn't want to go. Her nerves were still on fire wondering if he would have agreed had she asked.

Probably not. His loyalty to Ethan outweighed any desire for her. It would take time for Chase to trust her and he wouldn't advance things to the next level unless he was convinced she wouldn't burn him.

As she was rounding her car, a familiar form appeared across the street. She grinned in delight and waved.

"What are you doing here?" Chase asked, heading in her direction.

"I might ask you the same question," she countered with a mischievous smile. "I know Ethan wants you to keep an eye on me, but does it include stalking me all over Charleston?"

His gaze shifted to the Calloway house. "That's not why I'm here."

"No?" She arched a skeptical eyebrow.

For a long moment, Chase looked as if he was grappling with something. Then he gestured with his thumb toward the house directly across the street. "I live there."

Teagan couldn't believe her luck. "Seriously? Are you saying that we're going to be neighbors?" She beamed at him. "Does that mean I can pop over whenever I need to borrow a cup of sugar?"

Chase gave the matter some thought. "I'm not sure I have any sugar."

"What? Are you trying to tell me you're already sweet enough?"

"Honestly, Teagan," he exclaimed, but his exasperation seemed forced.

"Honestly, Chase." She took a step into his space and watched his nostrils flare. "You might look all tough and act all intimidating, but deep inside you're a cream puff." She set her finger against his unyielding chest and nudged. "A sweet, gooey cream puff."

He growled. "Cream puffs are not gooey."

"Maybe not, but they're sweet and my favorite dessert." She splayed her fingers over his heart and basked in the heat radiating off his sun-warmed skin. All of a sudden, she desperately wanted to be alone with him. "So, since we're about to be neighbors, don't you think you should be all neighborly and give me a tour of your house?"

His lashes flickered. "I was on my way out."

"I don't need to see the whole house." She leaned forward and whispered, "You can save your bedroom for another time."

He gave her such a stern look that she couldn't resist a giggle. The girlish sound coming out of her was a strange and marvelous thing. When it came to Chase, she never calculated what she said or how she behaved around him. Instead, she just went with her feelings of the moment and it was liberating to be herself, unshackled from others' expectations.

"Fine. A quick tour. It'll give you an idea of the quality of work I do."

They crossed the street and approached his house. The structure was long and narrow with a set of steps leading to a broad side porch and the front door. Teagan had only seconds to take in the neat boxwood planters flanking the entrance and the romantic porch swing before Chase ushered her through the double doors and into a cozy foyer.

Gleaming wide-plank heart pine floors led the way to a tranquil living room painted the palest sage green and decorated with a white sofa flanked by sapphire velvet armchairs. A dramatic seascape featuring various shades of blue and turquoise hung above the fireplace, but it was the beautiful molding details and fireplace surround that snagged her attention.

"The house was built in 1852," Chase narrated as he led the way across the hall to the large dining room and, without pausing, swept her into an enormous chef's kitchen. "At the time I bought it, this was the second-worst house on the block."

"That's certainly not the case anymore."

Although Teagan rarely fixed elaborate meals, she could see herself puttering around the big island, chopping fruit for her smoothies and assembling appetizers for happy hour on the back patio.

"I'm really in love with this kitchen. Having panels on the fridge and dishwasher gives the cabinets a seamless look. And this is…?" She smoothed her hand across the white countertop veined with gray.

"I chose quartz for its durability, but many of my clients have gone with marble."

"I can see we're going to have a lot to talk about," she told him, smiling wistfully. Design was her favorite part of the process and she couldn't wait to get going on the house across the street.

All too soon the tour was over.

For over a week now she'd been flirting madly with

Chase in an effort to find out if he was attracted to her. Yet, despite how many times she'd rehearsed these words in her mind, having the opportunity to speak them caught her flat-footed.

"There's something that's been on my mind," she told him as they stood in the foyer prior to exiting the house. Her breath hitched at the risk she was about to take.

One eyebrow rose but he gave her the space to speak her mind. This was another thing she appreciated about him. He actually listened to her. She was tired of men who either monopolized the conversation with stories about themselves or bombarded her with opinions about her favorite subjects.

Still, she'd be a fool not to recognize that the two of them couldn't be more different. Yet as drawn as she was to Chase's stoic strength, she wondered if anything about her appealed to him. Sure, he'd kissed her—a couple times in fact—but never once had he taken things a step further. Maybe she was imagining the chemistry between them and he wasn't attracted to her.

Although she was dying to touch him, she kept her hands clenched at her sides. Her hunger for Chase had built to a point where she could no longer flirt and tease in the hopes that he'd take a hint and kiss her again. The man's preferred way of communicating was blunt and direct, so maybe she needed to take the bull by the horns and speak plainly.

"I know you don't like me. Nor do you have any reason to be nice to me. But this thing between us…" Teagan was so short of breath she could barely get the words out. "The chemistry or attraction—whatever it is—I can't stop thinking about you. About *being* with you."

The confession was a wild wind that swept away Teagan's pride, leaving her bare beneath Chase's stony stare. Shivering with both terror and excitement, she scoured his implacable expression.

Boom. Boom. Boom. Please. Please. Please.

Each thunderous beat of her heart was a wordless plea for him to act. But the seconds ticked by and he remained rooted in place, fueling her anxiety. "Oh for heaven's sake," she snapped, sounding strangled and desperate. "Say something!"

"That's not a good idea."

Hysterical laughter vibrated in her throat. "You think I don't know that?"

"Ethan...wouldn't understand."

Would his loyalty to Ethan prove stronger than the heat between them? And if it did, would her longing for him fade or strengthen? Did she want Chase because she couldn't have him or did his passion for restoring historic homes make him her perfect match?

"It's between us." Teagan's heart fluttered as his eyebrows drew together. "You don't need to tell him."

"And how long do you expect me to keep it quiet?"

His question caught her off guard. "I'm sorry...?"

"What do you see happening between us?" he elaborated, his green eyes boring into her.

Unsure of his thoughts, Teagan scrambled for the answer that would satisfy him. "I thought I made that clear. You and me together in bed...or out of it. I'm not opposed to taking a few risks if that's what you're into." When her cheeky retort landed with a dull thud, Teagan pushed out a sigh. "I don't know how much clearer I can be. I want to have sex with you."

"And then what?"

"I don't know..." Teagan exhaled. Why did the man have to be so difficult? "Dinner might be nice."

Now it was Chase's turn to sigh. "I mean, where do you see this going?"

"Does it have to go anywhere?"

His scowl deepened. "So, all you're looking for is a distraction while you're in Charleston?"

Teagan's mouth dropped open. How had that been the conclusion he'd derived from her bold admission? Did he think she was some sort of mattress-hopping hedonist who used men and cast them aside?

"Why are you making this so complicated?" she grumbled. "I'm attracted to you and I think you're attracted to me. All I want is to spend some time exploring that." The way he'd forced her to explain herself was infuriating. Yet, she'd come too far to back down now. "We don't need to bring Ethan—or any other member of my family—into it." She flung up her hands in an uncharacteristically flamboyant gesture. "Look, if you're not interested, just say so and I'll never mention it again."

He was silent so long that she nearly fled in abject humiliation. What stopped her was a hot, fierce glow in his eyes that disabled her muscles and hampered her ability to move. Teagan's chest was too tight to draw a full breath so she stood before him, sipping air into her stalled lungs and growing dizzier by the moment.

"Chase—" His name on her lips was a husky plea.

Needing something solid to hold on to while her head spun, she reached out and set her fingertips on his muscular forearm.

"Fine. You want to know if I'm interested." His voice was husky, tortured even. "I'm interested."

Six

"Really?" She gasped as a quiver traveled down her lean length.

"Really."

Sparks exploded in her eyes, setting off an electrical overload of desire that sizzled and popped its way along his nerve endings. With his confession on the table between them, Chase expected her expression to reflect smug satisfaction at his agreement, but she looked more relieved than triumphant. Relieved that he hadn't rebuffed her? Was that even possible? Surely the confident Teagan Burns realized he'd been losing the battle with his libido from the moment they'd met.

When he considered the type of woman he usually dated, they were nothing like Teagan. If asked for a list of preferences, uncomplicated and sweet-natured would top his list. Teagan was multi-faceted, too clever for her own good, and provoking his discomfort energized her. Yet since their first encounter, she'd also defied his preconceived notion of her and surprised him over and over.

Chase lifted his hand and threaded his fingers through her long hair. He'd kissed her twice before, but not the way he wanted to. Not the way his body demanded. He was hungry for her. Starving. She, and only she, could put an end to this aching, empty feeling inside him.

"Then let's do this," she murmured, the intensity of her will hammering at him. "Now. Here."

Strong in her vulnerability. Determined in her desperation. She was powerful and yielding, complex and straightforward. Giving into this pull between them would end badly. Their opposite natures would eventually put them at odds. But Chase hadn't become a black belt without getting his ass kicked from time to time.

"You don't want me to take you to dinner first?" His amused tone belied the frantic need clawing at him.

She cocked her head and arched her eyebrows. "*This* is the moment you pick to show me you have a sense of humor?"

"I'm not trying to be funny."

Why was he still talking? He should just take her the way she'd asked him to. Here and now. Hard and fast against his front door and purge her from his system without making anything more of it. Instead, he was having visions of a romantic dinner at Husk, followed by a drive through the historic district. And after the anticipation had built to the shattering point, he would enjoy a long night of exploring exactly how hot she could burn.

"It's probably the genteel thing to do." She gave a husky laugh. "But there's no way I can wait that long."

As if to demonstrate just how needy she was, Teagan drove her slim body into his solid frame. Sucking in a lungful of her scent, his senses went on full alert. As he wrapped her in his arms, she lifted up on tiptoe and tunneled her fingers into his hair.

"Make love to me, Chase."

An intoxicating euphoria surged through his veins. His lips descended, claiming her mouth in a feverish kiss. A moan rose from deep inside his chest. Her slender form trembled as he pulled her close. Chase found his own body quaking as her lips parted and her tongue danced against his. The ache in his loins flared, but it was the spasm in his chest that spelled trouble.

Rational thought grew hazy as he kissed her deep and deeper still. She was a flickering flame in his arms, all heat and need. Catching fistfuls of his hair, she matched his hard kisses with fervent eagerness. Bit by bit the passion consuming him muted his doubts until there was only his blinding desire to possess her.

But not like this. Not here in his foyer. He wanted her in the middle of his bed where he'd imagined her so many times. Despite her height, she was light as a downy feather when he picked her up. Or maybe the need rampaging through him added additional fuel to his muscles. Chase took the stairs two at a time, arriving on the second-floor landing barely winded.

She wore a loose-fitting dress that he whisked over her head a second after her feet landed on his bedroom floor. Despite his heart's urgent drumming, Chase paused to look at her. Disheveled golden hair framed flushed cheeks and dancing green eyes. She smoothed her palm across his chest, no doubt to savor the frantic pounding of his heart. A slow, feline smile curved her lips.

"You look like you've never seen a woman before," she teased, reaching behind her to unfasten her bra.

"Never one like you," he breathed, his mouth going dry as she cast aside her lingerie and stood naked before him. "You're not just beautiful." He cupped her cheek, determined to soothe away the uncertainty that caused her to gnaw at her lower lip. "You're challenging and exciting one minute, and then funny and vulnerable the next. Sparring with you keeps me on my toes. I imagine the same will be said for making love with you."

She'd grown serious as he spoke, but her words remained playful. "I wouldn't want to disappoint."

He heard the plaintive call for reassurance and shook his head. "Impossible."

Her fingers traveled down the front of his shirt, plucking one button after another. Chase got to work on his belt and zipper. Soon, his clothes had joined hers on his floor. Before they came together, they stood, breathing hard, staring at each other.

"You are even more impressive without your clothes on." She smoothed the pads of her fingers across his chest while shaking her head in appreciative amazement. "I never imagined... Your chest. Your arms. Those abs." Her gaze drifted lower and one eyebrow shot up as she took in his jutting erection. "Wow." She expelled the last word in a breathless rush. "Just wow."

"You're staring at me like you've never seen a naked man before."

"I like funny Chase," she purred, taking his hand as she began easing backward. She stopped when her thighs hit the mattress and met his gaze. "He makes me feel at ease."

He cupped her breast, running his thumb across her tight nipple, and smiled when she gasped. Leaning down, he nuzzled her neck and murmured, "Want to hear the knock-knock joke Annabelle told me yesterday?"

"Later," she growled, her hand coming between them.

He'd barely recovered from the incendiary brush of her knuckles against his belly when she wrapped her long fingers around his hard length, ripping a muffled oath from him. He managed to suck in a single breath before his lungs stopped working. Closing his eyes, Chase covered her hand with his, savoring several seconds of excruciating bliss even as the wildness threatened to consume him. Gently pulling her fingers away, he pressed a lingering kiss into her palm, and then scooped her up and deposited her on the bed. He was upon her a second later, his lips riding the delicate column of her throat, nostrils drawing in her unique scent.

Her hands were busy on him, trailing fire across his shoulders, riding the terrain of his back muscles, driving her fingers into his hair. Pushing aside the siren call of her perfect breasts for the moment, Chase licked across her collarbone and nipped the strong cord in her neck.

When his lips reached her ear, he murmured, "I need you to come for me."

"I'm down for that."

Smiling at her eager response, Chase drew circles around her breast with his lips. Her body writhed in restless eagerness long before he settled his mouth over her nipple. At the same time he dusted caresses along her thigh. With each advancing inch of his fingertips, her quaking grew.

"Chase…"

Her breath came in shallow pants as he reached the place where her thighs came together. Moving with great care, he parted her feminine folds, seeking her wetness. Her lashes floated down as he slid his finger into her slippery heat, and he imagined how she would feel when he drove into her. Her hips bucked as he grazed her clit and circled it, paying attention to what made her moan, the hitches in her breath. She ground herself against his hand, swiveling and rocking as she chased her pleasure. As much as he wanted to join her so they could come together, it was equally wonderful to watch her shatter as an orgasm tore through her.

"I'm sorry," she said, her apology shocking him. "That was really fast." Closing her thighs, she pressed his palm tight against her as the last few waves of her climax pounded her. "It's been a while…a long while and I've been thinking about you—about this—ever since we met."

No words had ever sounded so perfect. "Ah, Teagan." Reluctant delight tinged his voice. "The things you do to me."

Chase kissed her hard then, feeling her skin melt into his. Electricity crackled between them, a powerful current of energy that created an endless, glorious connection. He nibbled his way down her neck, while his fingers coasted across the glorious swell of her breasts. She moaned when he circled her nipple with his tongue, and her back bowed as she thrust herself against his mouth, silently begging him for more.

"You are perfect." His voice was a raspy murmur

against her quivering abdomen as his tongue dipped into her navel before drifting across her hip bones.

"No. You are." She gasped the last word as his tongue followed the path his fingers had traveled earlier, trailing into her heat and causing her to shut her eyes and cry out. "I've already come once," she protested even as her fingers tunneled into his hair and pressed his mouth tight against her.

He liked the ravenous sounds she made. The way she offered herself to his pleasure. Her breaths came in desperate pants as he plied her with lips and tongue toward another orgasm.

"Chase," she keened his name and came hard against his mouth, growing hotter and wetter with each shattered cry. And still he kept on, settling into a rhythm she liked until her thighs spasmed and she launched into yet another climax.

Only when she lay panting and limp, her flushed face hidden behind long fingers, did he pluck a condom from the nightstand and tear it open. She lifted onto her elbows, her gaze hot and greedy as he slid it on. Noting the way she watched him, he grasped himself and gave several long, slow pumps, loving the way her eyes flared and her tongue slipped across her passion-bruised lower lip.

"Get over here, you gorgeous man," she commanded huskily, reaching for him. "I need you inside me now."

"I love a woman who knows what she wants," he said and then he was moving between her thighs, her softness yielding to his hard demand.

Her hand came between them, fingertips guiding his hard length to her soft heat. He rubbed the head of his erection against her and groaned. She set the soles

FREE BOOKS GIVEAWAY

GET UP TO FOUR FREE BOOKS & TWO FREE GIFTS WORTH OVER $20!

We pay for everything!

Dear Reader,

I am writing to announce the launch of a huge **FREE BOOKS GIVEAWAY**... and to let you know that YOU are entitled to choose up to FOUR fantastic books that WE pay for.

Try **Harlequin® Desire** books featuring the worlds of the American elite with juicy plot twists, delicious sensuality and intriguing scandal.

Try **Harlequin Presents® Larger-Print** books featuring the glamourous lives of royals and billionaires in a world of exotic locations, where passion knows no bounds.

Or **TRY BOTH!**

In return, we ask just one favor: Would you please participate in our brief Reader Survey? We'd love to hear from you.

This FREE BOOKS GIVEAWAY means that your introductory shipment is completely free, <u>even the shipping</u>! If you decide to continue, you can look forward to curated monthly shipments of brand-new books from your selected series, always at a discount off the cover price! <u>Plus you can cancel any time</u>. Who could pass up a deal like that?

Sincerely

Pam Powers

Pam Powers
For Harlequin Reader Service

Complete the survey below and return it today to receive up to 4 FREE BOOKS and FREE GIFTS guaranteed!

FREE BOOKS GIVEAWAY
Reader Survey

1

Do you prefer stories with happy endings?

◯ YES ◯ NO

2

Do you share your favorite books with friends?

◯ YES ◯ NO

3

Do you often choose to read instead of watching TV?

◯ YES ◯ NO

YES! Please send me my Free Rewards, consisting of **2 Free Books from each series I select** and **Free Mystery Gifts**. I understand that I am under no obligation to buy anything, no purchase necessary see terms and conditions for details.

❏ Harlequin Desire® (225/326 HDL GRK3)
❏ Harlequin Presents® Larger-Print (176/376 HDL GRK3)
❏ Try Both (225/326 & 176/376 HDL GRLF)

FIRST NAME | LAST NAME

ADDRESS

APT.# | CITY

STATE/PROV. | ZIP/POSTAL CODE

EMAIL ❏ Please check this box if you would like to receive newsletters and promotional emails from Harlequin Enterprises ULC and its affiliates. You can unsubscribe anytime.

of her feet on the mattress and pressed up so that he slipped a little way inside her.

"Teagan…" He kissed her and grappled with the lust raging inside him.

She skimmed her fingers over his abs and around to his back, murmuring a distracted, "Yes, Chase?"

"It's been a while for me, too."

"So take me quick and hard," she commanded in an urgent whisper. "We can take our time later."

Her fingernails sank into his naked butt, the sharp pain driving him into her. Intense pleasure shot up his spine. He hadn't realized he'd closed his eyes until a meteor shower blazed across his mind. A curse exploded from his lips as she laughed with pleasure. The joyful sound was almost as amazing as being inside her. She wriggled beneath him, tipping her hips to take him deeper.

He held himself suspended in her heat for several seconds until the raging in his blood reduced to a manageable simmer. Despite her urging to make this first time hot and fast, he wanted to make it perfect for her. With her lips against his ear, murmuring wicked phrases, he began to move inside her. Despite the need clawing at his body, Chase refused to yield his control. He wasn't going to take anything from her when all he wanted to do was to give.

So, he harnessed the discipline he'd learned through years of martial arts training and thrust into her with smooth, even strokes while remaining focused on the cues her body offered. The sounds she made, her moans, the staccato exhalations and the encouraging words spilling from her lips that told him to speed up, slow down or drive harder.

He wasn't surprised that she knew what she liked and how to get it. She'd always been direct. In bed it was no different. The way she wrapped her legs around his waist and held herself tight against him drove him toward his own explosive orgasm. He loved how she rocked and ground against him while sexy, helpless noises erupted from her lips.

With his own pleasure building into a smoking volcano, he could no longer tell if his lungs were working properly. They surged together, finding a frantic pace that stripped them down to male and female. There was no more Teagan and Chase. Only hands and skin, heat and friction.

Sweat broke out on his skin as lust began to short-circuit his brain. He had to hold on. She was so close. But he was closer.

Chase ground his teeth and growled, "Come for me."

"You first."

Damn the stubborn woman.

"Come now, Teagan." He slid his hand beneath her butt and held her as he slammed into her.

She emitted a startled moan as the first ripple of her climax took hold of her. With his last thread of willpower, he held off his release for a few frantic heartbeats so he could watch her come. He wanted to imprint the memory of her eyes glazing over and the transformation of her face as her expression shifted from focused concentration to euphoria. He'd never seen a woman surrender to pleasure like that and it was only then, amidst this moment of profound intimacy, that he allowed himself to be swept off the cliff into his own concussive orgasm.

In the aftermath, Chase lay on his back, staring at the ceiling while Teagan's breath puffed against his chest.

The contentment spreading through his body left him grappling with the consequences of letting Teagan in. He knew better than to trust her and recognized that any relationship with her wouldn't be easy.

But this woman shared his passion for restoration and in bed she'd proved both bold and enthusiastic. He recognized that his appetite for her was a deep well that might never run dry.

The stark, terrifying reality was that Teagan Burns was his match in every way, the partner he never knew he needed and the dream girl he'd never seen coming.

During the days following his first night with Teagan, Chase noticed himself falling deeper beneath her spell. Thoughts of her consumed him during the day when he was supposed to be working, and at night he spent endless hours with her in his bed, learning every inch of her skin, what drove her wild and the limitless power of their passion for each other.

He should've been glad that she'd headed off to New York to deal with some issues that had arisen in her absence. Time apart was the ideal solution to his bewitchment. Distance would allow his head to clear and reason to reassert itself.

Instead, he'd been plagued by a raging ache for her kisses and a gut-churning loneliness that only her intoxicating presence eased. The lingering scent of her on his sheets and his discovery of a pair of her black lace panties beneath his bed kept memories of her fresh in his mind. As did the rapid-fire exchange of text messages that began when he woke and continued long into the night. She'd invaded his life so seamlessly that it seemed impossible that they'd known each other less than two weeks.

On the morning of the third day without Teagan, Chase was on a job site when his phone rang. Excusing himself from the general contractor, he answered the call.

"Where are you?" Sawyer asked, sounding tense and unhappy.

"The Carlson job."

"Is that the one on Montague?"

"Yes."

"I'm five minutes away."

She hung up on him before Chase had a chance to ask her what was wrong. At least he didn't have to wait long for the explanation. He had just enough time to wrap up the final punch list items before her car arrived at the curb.

Sawyer exited her car and waited for him on the sidewalk. As he approached, he noticed the way her appreciative gaze trailed over the updated facade. "Wow, that looks amazing."

"Thank you. So, what's up?"

"We might have a problem."

"You've just described my average day," he quipped, realizing Teagan's habitual bantering was rubbing off on him. "What's happened?"

"There's another offer on the Calloway property."

"Damn!" Chase's gut tightened at this unwelcome news.

"I know. Crazy, right?"

"Crazy," Chase echoed, thinking of all the months it had sat on the market when Rufus had tried to sell it before. "And unexpected. It's never stirred anyone's interest before and now there are two people vying for it."

"It is surprising," Sawyer agreed.

Rufus had a knack for ruining perfectly sound businesses by throwing money at inventive opportunities that never worked out, which was why he was once again keen to sell the Calloway house. It was also why a lucrative offer might override his determination to do right by a house that had once been in his family.

Chase visualized a worst-case scenario. If Teagan didn't get the house, there was a real possibility that his mother's ancestral home might go to someone who only saw the value in the large lot in the heart of downtown Charleston. Maybelle would be devastated if the home was destroyed.

"Have you told Teagan?" Chase asked, imagining her disappointment.

"I called, but she didn't pick up, so I left a message." Sawyer looked worried. "She put in a solid offer—above asking—so I think she should be okay, but I thought if she also wrote a letter explaining how she wants to offer the three houses on the property to at-risk women that he might be swayed to let her have the house."

"Do you think it will work?" Chase didn't want to come off as pessimistic, but his cousin had never been particularly altruistic. If the other offer was stronger than Teagan's, they ran the risk of losing the property.

Teagan's passion for the project had intensified Chase's already keen enthusiasm. Two years ago, Rufus had put the house on the market and Chase had envisioned securing the property and undertaking an extensive renovation. When Rufus realized Chase and his family were the only interested parties, he'd cancelled the listing. Since then, Chase felt as if he had a vested interest in seeing that the renovation was done to his exacting standards. In addition, because the house was across the street from his own home, he'd be constantly aggravated if the construction was subpar.

"Time will tell," Sawyer said. "Rufus might be swayed by a generous offer, but I can't imagine anyone paying more than what Teagan offered." She held her hands palm up in a helpless gesture.

"Does he know she intends to work with me?"

"Not that I know of. It might help if you avoided her until we're under contract, but given what Ethan wants you to do that seems impossible."

"I'm really between a rock and a hard place on this whole affair," Chase grumbled, wondering how his life had gotten so complicated when all he'd thought to do this summer was be left in peace to complete his current projects and prepare for the Carolopolis Awards. "Do you think you could find out who the other buyer is?"

Although offers were usually anonymous, sometimes an agent dropped a little tidbit about their client. Chase was alive with curiosity and concern.

"Funny you should ask…" Sawyer gave him a sly smile. "Rufus listed the property with a guy who works out of the same brokerage as Emmett." Emmett Morris was Sawyer's second cousin and if anyone could persuade him to reveal juicy tidbits it was her. "I thought you might be interested in listening in as I give him a call."

Chase leaned against the hood of Sawyer's car and crossed his arms. "Let's do it."

"I was hoping you'd say that." Sawyer must've been just as worked up about the competitive offer as Chase because her body hummed with a jittery energy as she cued up a number and put the phone on speaker.

"Hey, cuz." Emmett's nasally tenor sounded genuinely happy to hear from Sawyer. "How are things with you?"

"On the whole, pretty good. How about you?"

"We're in real estate, darlin'. It's a mad mad world. But you know that."

"I do." Both cousins chuckled. "Hey, look, I was wondering if you could help me out. I have a client who put in an offer on Rufus Calloway's old place."

"I heard. Although I can't imagine why anyone, much less two anyones, would be interested in that eyesore."

Sawyer shot an apologetic glance Chase's way, but he merely waved off her concern.

"I can't speak for the other interested party, but my buyer has been looking for a historic home in need of work. She's dying to restore the property and turn the cottages out back into transitional housing for domestic abuse victims."

"Phil-an-thro-py," Emmett declared and Chase could imagine him nodding enthusiastically. "I can get behind that."

"So, you can see why she's freaked out that someone else is interested in the property. Is there anything you know about the other buyer?"

"Not much. I did hear that the guy's from New York, though."

This news gave Chase a jolt. He would've preferred someone local who could appreciate the home's value was not just in the location, but also its history. What were the chances that someone else from New York would be as passionate about restoration as Teagan?

"Wow! New York. That's where my buyer's from, too." Sawyer turned a confused look on Chase. "Who would've guessed that the Calloway property would entice buyers from so far away?"

"I don't know why you're surprised," Emmett said. "Seems like there's more and more outside money moving into Charleston every month."

And to Chase's mind, not always for the better. He worried that in their determination to occupy one of the prestigious historic homes in and around downtown Charleston that outsiders would fail to appreciate the artisan details as well as the dings and flaws that represented the home's long history. How many heart pine floors had been torn up to make way for manufactured hardwood or original fixtures tossed out as contemporary bathrooms were added?

"As I mentioned, my client is interested in restoring the property," Sawyer continued. "I don't suppose you have any sense what the other party intends to do."

"I didn't hear, but I can dig into it a bit if you want."

Sawyer raised her eyebrows at Chase and he nodded.

"It would be great if you could."

"I do know one thing. The other offer was really good."

Higher than what Teagan had offered? This didn't bode well. If Rufus was seeing dollar signs, he might be blind to what would become of his great-aunt Maybelle's childhood home.

"Over asking?" Sawyer prompted.

"Definitely."

Chase recalled Teagan's hungry gaze as she'd toured

the property. He'd recognized that look. It reflected his own eagerness every time he took a project from disastrous to dynamic. In his career he'd taken a lot of risks. Not all of them had paid off financially, but the satisfaction in a job well done had outweighed the hit to his bottom line.

He eyed Sawyer as she ended the call. "What do you think?"

"I don't want to be pessimistic," she replied, her blue-grey eyes clouded with worry. "But this could be a problem."

Seven

On the third day of her New York visit, Teagan met her mother in their fashion line's design studio.

"Well, it's about time you came home," her mother said, not attempting to sugar-coat her displeasure.

Was New York home? Teagan wasn't sure anymore. More and more and despite the mess she'd made, she envisioned her future in Charleston. It's where her birth mother had grown up and the city was steeped in her family's history.

And then there was Chase. She'd never known anyone like him. After only two days in New York, she missed him terribly. He'd surprised her as a lover, demonstrating that fierce passion simmered beneath his flinty demeanor. Given how he'd resisted her in the beginning and made it clear that he wasn't keen on being attracted to her, once he'd decided to surrender to the incandescent chemistry between them, he'd given her everything.

Her skin tingled as she recalled his impassioned groans and delighted sighs as his powerful body had driven her to the stars. Each time he'd been so tuned into her every need. His consideration had only increased her desire and made her appreciate him all the more.

Never before Chase had Teagan been with a man who cherished her. Feeling safe had allowed her to be vulnerable with him and their deep intimacy transformed her.

"We need to talk about the designs for our Spring line," her mother said, referring to the clothing company they'd started the year Teagan turned thirteen.

While the line bore Teagan's name and the designs were shaped by her creativity, Anna Burns was the driving force behind the company—especially in the early years when Teagan just wanted to be photographed and admired wearing pretty clothes.

"Of course," Teagan agreed. "And while we're discussing it, I wanted to let you know that I plan on opening a boutique in Charleston."

Her mother made a derisive sound. "Why?"

"My roots are in Charleston and I intend to establish myself there." The fervent declaration surprised her until Teagan realized that she spoke with her whole heart.

"Your mother left Charleston," Anna reminded her. "She came to New York to establish herself here. Why would you want to go backwards?"

Teagan didn't consider embracing her Charleston roots to be a step backwards. "I have family there."

"I thought we were your family."

"You are." Uttering those two words didn't reverse the way Teagan had been feeling since learning her father had no intention of turning the family business over to a girl he'd adopted. "But they are, too. And I want to get to know them better."

Anna Burns sniffed. "You have a life here. Businesses. Responsibilities. Friends. Why are you wasting your time in Charleston?"

"I don't feel like I'm wasting my time." But she hadn't exactly been successful thus far. Still, running back to Manhattan with her tail between her legs wasn't the answer either. She'd learn from her failures and avoid making the same mistakes.

In her heart of hearts she knew that she had gone down to Charleston in the hope of winning everyone to her side. She wanted to be embraced as one of them, and though she'd made a mess of things, she just needed a little more time to fix what she'd broken.

The Calloway house was a symbol of this next step. She would take something broken and bring it back to life. And in the process, she would prove she belonged in Charleston. A year from now she would be hosting friends and family and aiding women who needed help. Her vision left her feeling satisfied and at peace, a very different sensation than she'd known until now.

In New York she was constantly vying for the limelight. Even her most charitable moments were captured and posted for the world to see. It left Teagan wondering if she was actually doing good or just looking as if she was doing good for the cameras. She wanted more substance in her life.

The urge to pick up her phone and call Chase seized

her while Anna was showing her swatches of the fabric under consideration. Everything about him appealed to her. Despite their rocky start, was she thinking the way she was because of how he challenged her? Or was he influencing her by just being who he was?

Swept by the need to connect with him, she composed and sent a text.

How are the revised plans for the house coming?

She'd taken a business tone with him because what she really wanted to ask him terrified her. Did he miss her? Because her body ached for him. She was now seeing her future through fresh eyes, and that future included more days and nights with Chase. Her blood sang its need to feel his breath warming her skin, for his hands to grip and guide her body to the most acute pleasure she'd ever experienced.

To her astonishment, he replied almost immediately.

I spent last night making the changes you requested.

This filled her with a significant amount of delight.

So you were thinking about me last night. That sounds nice.

This was the exact sort of flirtation that annoyed him, but she was starting to think that despite his grumbling, he might like it a little. In any case, the flirtation was a terrific way to mask her fear of his rejection.

I think I've included everything we talked about.

Always the professional. Suddenly, she wanted to rattle his calm and get past his walled exterior. His kisses told her that he wasn't as unaffected as he acted most of the time. That her touch drove him wild. That their sexual chemistry was mutual. Just the thought excited her because her insides fluttered with delight whenever he was near. She was good at reading people and couldn't reconcile how he could seem so unaffected and then kiss her with such exquisite fervor.

I've been missing you.

Sending such a revealing declaration was a risk, but as she'd learned long ago, no risk, no reward. Still, she felt like her heart had shrunk to the size of a pea before he responded.

You've been on my mind a lot. When are you coming back to Charleston?

It wasn't a declaration of undying affection, but for someone like Chase, admitting even this much must've been difficult. And that he wanted a return date made her eager to complete her business and rush back to him.

Since it's obvious we can't stand to be apart, I'm going to cut my trip short. I'll be back the day after tomorrow.

Another lengthy pause followed her text. Was he regretting giving her a glimpse into his psyche? Her hammering heart left her breathless as she awaited his reply.

Send me your flight information and I'll pick you up.

This response leveled Teagan. She never imagined he would put himself out for her. Part of her knew that it was probably his Southern manners taking over, but another more hopeful part of her wanted to trust that he had feelings for her.

Thank you. I'll let you know when I have the information.

She wondered if this was too cool a response, but then he replied with a thumbs-up emoji and she was enchanted all over again. Damn the man for surprising her at every turn. She might've been able to keep her wits about her if he hadn't demonstrated such adorable gallantry.

"Teagan!"

Her mother's impatient call snapped Teagan out of her reverie. She quickly scanned the designs and fabrics before making her selections. In five minutes she'd determined the spring line and aimed a smile at her mother.

"There," she said. "That should be a wonderful collection. Don't you think?"

Without waiting for Anna to agree, Teagan picked up her purse and headed for the door. She had two more stops to make and several appointments to cancel since she'd decided to cut her trip short.

As she pushed through the building's main entrance and made her way across the sidewalk to hail a cab, a limo glided to a stop before her. A darkened window lowered in dramatic fashion, revealing the sculpted lines of Declan Scott's smug face.

"Are you stalking me?" she demanded, hiding her disquiet behind sarcasm.

Why could she never seem to anticipate Declan's moves? Each time he caught her off guard was a skirmish he won and she was so weary of losing to him all the time.

"Let's just say you make it very easy to bump into you."

Teagan knew at once what he meant. Her Instagram account. She tried to tag the local restaurants and shops as much as possible to give the businesses she visited some social media exposure. As she'd arrived at the design studio, she'd paused in the foyer to take a selfie beside the Teagan Burns fashion logo in order to stimulate interest in their upcoming fall collection.

"If I'd known you were using it to track me, I would've stopped broadcasting my location." She leveled an unfriendly glower at him. "Don't you have things to do? Why are you here hassling me?"

"I signed some paperwork for a new property I intend to acquire and thought you might be interested in having a drink with me to celebrate."

"Let me guess, you found another historic gem in Midtown that you can't wait to tear down."

"It is historic, but I wouldn't exactly call it a gem." Declan paused for a beat. "And it's quite a bit farther south than Midtown."

Teagan noted Declan's smug satisfaction and braced herself for the blow. They'd engaged in enough skirmishes over the years for her to recognize that he was holding a winning hand.

"Good luck with it."

With those parting words, she pivoted and headed

off to hail a taxi. She hadn't taken more than two steps before she heard the sound of a car door slamming behind her. A moment later, Declan caught her arm and spun her to face him.

"I don't have time for this," she ground out, shaking off his hand. "I'm late for an appointment." A lie, but he wasn't listening to her anyway.

"Come have a drink with me." The predatory glee in his eyes made Teagan grind her teeth. "Aren't you at all curious about the property I'm so eager to buy?"

"Not in the least."

"You should be."

His dark warning made her shiver. "I'm no longer interested in New York real estate. I'm shifting my focus to Charleston."

"So am I."

The malice on Declan's face sent her anxiety spiking through the roof. She stared at him with rising dread.

"What do you mean?" But she was pretty sure she'd already figured it out.

"Turns out that you are not the only buyer interested in the Calloway property."

Ruthless, arrogant bastard.

"You…" Any further words were strangled by a massive lump forming in her throat.

"Rufus Calloway was very excited about my offer." He paused to let that sink in before twisting the knife. "It's double the asking price."

"I can match that," she told him. "And I'll let him know that I plan to offer the three cottages on the property as transitional housing for domestic abuse victims."

"I'm sure you'll write a charming letter detailing all the good you plan to do for Charleston, but I'm guessing Calloway won't give a damn about your sentimental blathering."

Teagan's heart gave a desperate lurch. "You don't know that."

"Also," Declan added, acting as if he hadn't heard her, "I considered the possibility that you might try to outbid me so I let him know that you are colluding with Chase Love and intend to turn around and sell the house to him and his mother."

"That's not true." The urge to scream tore at her throat.

"Isn't it? From what I've heard you two have gotten quite close. Why wouldn't you sell your boyfriend the property his mother has been after for years?"

The thought that Declan had been spying on her and Chase made Teagan sick, but she couldn't let Declan know that he'd upset her.

Pushing down all her anxiety, Teagan summoned her best nonchalant shrug and met his gaze. "While I will admit I was quite taken with the Calloway property, it isn't the only property in Charleston that will work. I'll find another. And if you go after that one, I'll seek out another. You're going to spend a lot of time and money beating me out of every single house I look at."

"But I don't need to beat you out of every property. I just need to beat you out of this one. Because it's rather significant to your new lover, isn't it?"

Of course. Declan had done his research. No doubt he knew exactly how important the house was to Chase. Once again Declan had struck at someone Teagan cared about in order to get at her.

"Just sell me the Brookfield Building, Teagan. And

prevent your boyfriend's family home from being razed to the ground."

"You can't do that," she cried, panic getting the best of her as she imagined what a waste that would be.

"I can and I will." Declan gave a merciless laugh. "I told you what it will take for me to leave you alone."

"Edward never sold you the Brookfield Building and I won't either." Brave words, but could she really afford to keep the promise she'd made to her dead father?

"Edward," Declan scoffed. "You don't seriously think he gave a damn about you, do you?"

For a panicked moment, Teagan wondered if Declan knew the true nature of her connection to Edward Quinn. He could do a lot of damage with that information.

"Edward left you the building because he filled your head with ridiculous notions of saving Manhattan's architectural gems. And he knew you were one of the few people brave enough to take me on."

Even through her relief, Declan's words lashed at her, exacerbating the insecurity she'd grappled with since learning Edward was her father. Of course he hadn't cared for her. If he had, he would have claimed her. Instead, she suspected he'd been the one who'd arranged for her to be adopted by the Burns family. Had he known about Ava's family in Charleston? If he had, would he have returned her to the Watts family? What would her life have been like if she had grown up surrounded by her Charleston relatives, loved and appreciated? Teagan couldn't help but think she would've been a completely different person. Someone worthy of love.

"Well, you're right on one account," Teagan said, all too aware that if Declan didn't get his way, he would hound her all the rest of her days. "I am more than happy to take you on."

"Maybe for the moment." Declan looked utterly unruffled by her challenge. "But will you still feel the same after I've taken everything away from you?"

The disquiet that had plagued Chase during Teagan's absence was replaced by rumbling pleasure as she strolled through the sliding glass Arrivals door and headed straight to where he stood beside his SUV. The unbridled pleasure of her smile the instant she spotted him awakened a familiar hunger in him.

As soon as she drew within arm's reach, he stepped forward, wrapped his arm around her and claimed her lips in a sizzling kiss that betrayed just how much he'd missed her. She kissed him back with equal enthusiasm, proclaiming her own delight at their reunion. They were both breathing raggedly by the time he broke off the kiss. He surveyed her flushed cheeks with satisfaction as he escorted her into the passenger seat before stowing her carry-on.

He'd barely merged onto the interstate, heading south toward downtown, when he asked, "Are you available to have lunch with my mother?"

"But we've only been dating a couple of weeks." Teagan widened her eyes in a dramatic fashion while a sassy half smile teased at the corner of her lips. "Isn't it a little soon to bring me home?"

Despite knowing she was playing with him, Chase's gut tightened. He reminded himself that they weren't dating. A couple of dinners and the fact that he couldn't keep his hands or his lips to himself didn't mean anything romantic was happening between them. He was simply doing his best friend a favor by taking her out. As for all the fantastic sex… That was a little harder to justify. After all, Teagan was a beautiful, seductive woman who flirted with him at every opportunity. And he was a red-blooded male with little immunity. In fact, the only thing that cooled his libido was when he questioned whether her scheming ways were a thing of the past.

So what explanation could he rally for how he'd missed talking to her this past week while she was in New York? With her absent from Charleston, he should've been able to focus completely on work. Instead, he'd caught his attention straying too often to his phone, as if he could manifest a call or text from Teagan.

"She wants to talk to you about the Calloway house," Chase said, his chaotic thoughts making his tone brusque. "And your plans for the property."

"Did you tell her about the other offer?" Teagan asked, her voice suddenly low and tight.

"I mentioned that someone else has shown interest in the property." Chase tried to keep tension out of his voice as he added, "The other buyer is from New York."

"Sawyer mentioned that." Teagan stiffened a bit, then huffed out a laugh. "I guess I'm not the only one who thinks Charleston is a great investment."

"Of course. We get a lot of people from out of town interested in obtaining property in the downtown area," he said. "It's just that the renovation on the Calloway property is a major undertaking. You'd think they'd want something that carried less risk."

Though her expression was tight, Teagan gave a

single-shoulder shrug. "It's an amazing property in a wonderful neighborhood."

Something about her demeanor was off. Chase couldn't quite put his finger on it. He suspected she was worried that she might lose the Calloway property, yet she was covering it up with false bravado. She might just be trying to ease his concerns or convince herself to remain optimistic.

"So, lunch with your mom," she declared in overly bright tones. "When did you have in mind?"

"Does tomorrow work for you?"

"I'm free. But will it work for you?"

Her question confused him. "What do you mean?"

"I'm only asking because you refused to have lunch with me when we first met," she said. "Claiming that you were too busy."

"Why are you assuming I'd be there?"

He often used work as an excuse to avoid social situations, but Teagan was the first person to call him out on it.

"You couldn't possibly allow me to meet your mother alone." She knew him too well.

"It's lunch with my mother," he said, giving in. "I always make time for her."

"Seems like you make time for all the women in your life. Your sister. Your nieces. Your mother."

She hummed with approval, but it was her knowing smile as she deliberately didn't include herself in the list that caused his heartbeat to skip. Because he was making time for her in his life. A great deal of time.

"It's the way I was raised."

"And one of the things I find most attractive about

you." Her gaze did a slow, heated tour of his body, leaving little doubt what else she liked about him.

Usually when women flirted with him, Chase found the frivolous banter tiresome. He preferred his conversations straightforward. Having a meaningful dialog that exchanged opinions or shared facts or stories was more up his alley.

In Teagan's case, he suspected that she recognized his disdain for small talk and was pushing his buttons. The more he dug in and refused to answer in kind, the brighter her smiles and more provocative her words. She was a vexing woman, yet he couldn't shed his craving to be with her.

"So, lunch?" he growled at her.

"Tell your mother I'd love to," Teagan said, abruptly serious. "What time will you pick me up?"

Chase frowned at her. Why was she interpreting lunch with his mother to discuss the Calloway house as anything other than a business meeting? "I thought maybe we could meet there."

"Come now," she teased. "What happened to your Southern manners? Your mother invited me to lunch. Obviously, she's curious about the woman you've been seeing. Don't you think you should pick me up?"

"I might be coming from a job site and…" Chase knew if he overreacted, she would've won. "Fine," he grumbled. "I'll pick you up at twelve fifteen."

"I'll be waiting."

And she was. He arrived promptly at the time they'd arranged and before he'd shifted his SUV into park outside the front door of her grandfather's mansion, she was descending the curved front steps. With his gaze riveted on her, Chase exited the vehicle and raced to open the passenger door. She seemed to enjoy his chivalry as much as he enjoyed treating her like his special lady.

"How do I look?" Her green eyes sparkled demurely up at him from beneath her long lashes.

Today she wore a fluttery floral dress in peach tones with a purse and strappy heels to match. It was the perfect outfit to dine with his mother. Maybelle was going to love her. Curse it all.

"My mother will be enchanted," he declared in matter-of-fact tones as he gestured her into the passenger seat.

"And you?" Teagan stepped into his space, bringing with her the scent of jasmine. Her fingertips rested lightly on his forearm and the warmth of her seared through his fine cotton shirt. "Have I enchanted you as well?"

A slight catch in her soft voice tickled his nerve endings. It was all Chase could do not to wrap his arm around her waist and demonstrate her powerful effect on him. This was just another version of the same game. He couldn't be bamboozled by her change in tactics.

"Does it matter?" he countered, drowning in the need to cup her flushed cheek and revisit the delicious texture of her lips, the soft moans she made when he took her lower lip between his teeth. "It's my mother you need to impress."

"But it's you that I dressed for." Her fingers clutched at his sleeve. There was no flirtation in her manner, just openness and honesty. "I want you to find me attractive."

"You already know I do," he said slowly as if he could

somehow avoid the trap she'd laid for him. "You are the most beautiful woman I've ever seen."

She sighed and looked disappointed. "I think if I was an original marble fireplace, you'd be more enthusiastic."

He almost smiled at that. She knew him too well.

"You know you're beautiful," he said. "Why does my describing you that way disagree with you?"

"Because beauty isn't enough." Abruptly, she let her hand fall away from his arm. "When I said I want you to find me attractive, I mean that you find *me* attractive. Not just the exterior but what's in here and here." She pointed to her head and her heart. "I can't take credit for being beautiful. My drive, intelligence and ability to make things happen has always played second to my pretty face and blonde hair."

Her passionate declaration enabled Chase to better understand what drove her. "If you want me to value what's inside you, then why don't you stop toying with me?"

Teagan's eyes went wide and Chase wondered if he'd been too blunt. A second later, she burst out laughing. "So, what I'm hearing from you is that you'd like me to be more direct?"

Why did he feel as if he'd stepped from the frying pan into the fire? "It would help if I knew what was going on in that beautiful head of yours."

"I'll think about that," Teagan said, actually sounding as if she meant it. "In the meantime, why don't we head to your mother's house for lunch. I don't want to make a bad impression by being late."

Minutes later, as they walked hand in hand up the

steps that led to his mother's broad front porch, Teagan grew more somber. In fact, she looked positively grim.

"Relax." He gave her hand a gentle squeeze. My mother said she's been looking forward to seeing you for a while now. She approves of what you want to do with the Calloway property."

"She won't mind that I want to use it to help women in need?"

"That's part of why she's so delighted to have you developing the property."

"I'm glad to hear it. I imagine she's very disappointed that she can't buy the house herself."

"My mother is equal parts determined and practical. She was willing to do whatever we could to buy the house from Rufus. But she's not taking things to unreasonable extremes. She'd rather the home be purchased by someone who can appreciate it."

Teagan's gaze suddenly averted, but not before Chase spotted a flicker of something that triggered his uneasiness. He knew that she was accustomed to going it alone and that in times of stress, she regressed into familiar patterns. He could only hope that she wasn't concocting some mad plan that might blow up in their faces.

"What if I don't get it?" Teagan's voice was so soft it was almost a whisper. Her eyes held a haunted anxiety when she finally looked at him. "Will your mother hate me?"

It was a sign of her strength and her willingness to be vulnerable with him that she was able to voice her fears.

Moved, Chase reached out a hand to cup her cheek. "She could never hate you for something out of your control. Real estate is a tough business. Especially in a market like this one. And dealing with Rufus is tricky. My mother understands that."

Seeing that his reassuring words hadn't had their desired effect, he wrapped his other arm around her waist and pulled her close. Dipping his head, he captured her lips in a searing kiss that made the world fall away. Her hands dug into his back as she returned the kiss with blazing heat. They stood that way on the shady porch until someone cleared their throat.

Chase was breathing hard as he broke off the kiss. Glancing toward his mother's housekeeper, he noted her fond grin and offered her a cheeky wink.

"Your mother's been asking after you," she said, her voice dripping with amusement. "Shall I tell her you need a few more minutes so you can…wrap this up?"

"Oh, no," Teagan exclaimed, breaking free from Chase and running her hands along her skirt. "I mean we can certainly finish…our conversation later."

"Of course. Come in."

Chase was grinning broadly as he set his hand into the small of Teagan's back and escorted her across the threshold. Seeing the always-in-control Teagan Burns flustered was something he relished.

The housekeeper escorted them into the living room where his mother was busily typing on her smartphone. As he crossed the room with Teagan, Maybelle set the phone down and rose to greet them. His mother wore a linen suit in pale rose with a silk floral scarf around her neck. She ran an appraising look over the new arrivals before giving an approving nod.

"You must be Teagan," his mother said, holding out both hands in welcome. "My son is quite taken with you."

Although Chase wished his mother hadn't led with that, he had to agree that was the case.

"I don't know if he's taken with me." Teagan took his mother's hands in hers, looking pleased. "But I do believe I've convinced him to like me a little."

Maybelle shot her son a sharp glance. "Oh, I think he likes you more than a little. Especially given the clinch I saw on my front porch."

Chase sensed that if Teagan's hands had been free they would've been clapped over her burning cheeks. His own skin had grown uncomfortably warm. Well, what did he expect when he'd kissed Teagan like that at his mother's front door? And of course Maybelle would be avidly curious about the woman who'd captured his interest, since his mother had given up on seeing her workaholic son fall in love.

"You have a beautiful home," Teagan said as Maybelle led the way into the dining room. "I understand helping to restore it is what triggered Chase's love of architecture."

"It certainly did. Until then I thought he was going to open a martial arts studio. He earned his black belt at age fifteen and it was all he talked about. That changed after my husband died. Even though he was only seventeen, Chase stepped up and became the man of the family."

"At such a young age." Teagan gave her head a slow, sorrowful shake.

"Yes, Chase has always been so strong. He took such good care of us during those hard times." His mother glanced his way. "He still does."

Normally Chase would be put out listening to a pair of women discussing him as if he wasn't sitting at the same table. Instead, he was oddly charmed by the way his mother and Teagan had taken to each other.

"I've seen firsthand how good he is with children," Teagan said. "Makes me wonder why he never got married and started a family of his own."

"My guess is he's been too busy working," Maybelle replied. "I think all he needs is someone who shares his passion for restoring historic homes and can jolt him out of his routines."

Maybelle's summary left Teagan looking less delighted and more like a trapped animal. Her smile didn't quite reach her eyes as she declared, "Seems like I meet both of those requirements."

"I hope so." Maybelle reached over and patted her son's hand. "I'd like to see him with someone who makes him happy."

"Especially now that Ethan's getting married," Maybelle continued. "The two of them were thick as thieves since they were young."

"It's really wonderful that my sister and Ethan found each other." Teagan's expression had grown pensive. "He makes her so happy."

"Sounds like it's just as fortunate that my great-great-grandfather's house brought you and Chase together."

"I hope so," Teagan said, glancing his way, her serious eyes assessing his thoughts on the matter. When he gave her a reassuring nod, she exhaled and offered him a tremulous smile. "I know I'm really glad it did."

Eight

"That went well," Chase remarked, his tone neutral as he drove them back to his place.

Was he worried it had gone too well?

Not since he'd first brought it up had they discussed his promise to keep an eye on her for Ethan. Was Chase anticipating their growing closeness might cause a problem between him and his best friend? A painful knot formed in her chest. Would his loyalty to Ethan wrench him away from her?

Or would her own actions be to blame?

Teagan had been vacillating between guilt and giddy euphoria at his mother's warm welcome. She knew she should tell Chase that Declan had put in the competing bid for the Calloway property, but she feared once Chase found out, he wouldn't want to have anything to do with her anymore. The thought of losing him tore at her.

Except for her quick trip to New York City, they'd spent every night together. She'd never fallen for anyone this fast. She was consumed with Chase. His powerful body had become her playground, all those delicious muscles a never-ending source of blissful delights. She melted every time he held her face with his tender fingers and kissed her. And she relished how they spent hours necking on his couch, their hands sliding over clothes, letting anticipation build as they learned what each other liked. They were slowly forging a connection that went beyond lust or physical need, and with every day that ticked by, Teagan fell harder.

Which made her dread the looming storm on the horizon all that much more. Meeting his mother today had brought all her fears to the surface. Past experience told her to bury her agitation. She would just have to fix what was going on with Declan and keep Chase and his family from discovering the danger to their ancestral home. Would she be able to figure out how to best Declan before the truth came out and her tranquil little world became a hurricane of accusation and blame?

There was only one answer. She had to.

"I really like your mother," she said, forcing her thoughts back to Declan's comment.

"She likes you, too."

His opinion made her jubilant. "You can tell?"

"I can."

The approval radiating off him made her want to tear off his clothes and devour him. Fortunately there wasn't a lot of traffic and the distance between the houses owned by mother and son wasn't more than a few miles. They were already holding hands so all she had to do was raise his knuckles to her lips and nibble suggestively. He glanced at her, his hazel eyes kindling.

"I want you," she told him.

"I want you, too," he answered with a wolfish smile.

Loosening his grip on her hand, without releasing her entirely, he trailed the tips of his fingers beneath her dress and up her bare thigh. Teagan swallowed hard, her thighs falling apart to give him the access they both craved. He brushed the pads of his fingers across the crotch of her panties and sucked in his breath.

"You're wet," he remarked smoothly, his deep voice stroking her nerve endings, making her shudder.

"I'm hot for you" she answered, her voice not as steady as his. She'd never hidden her susceptibility to him. Why bother when her responsiveness aroused him? And she liked turning him on. "At home, I intend to encourage you to do all sorts of sexy things to me."

"I like the sound of that." Once again, his finger glided over her most sensitive area.

A low moan escaped her throat as she pressed his hand against her. When had she become so raw and needy?

"Aren't we there yet?" she whined, making the corners of his lips twitch.

He was so beautiful when he smiled. As much as she loved his smolder, the sheer joy in his laughter fired a longing to make him happy. Too bad it wasn't her destiny to live an uncomplicated life. This time she'd been with Chase was just a momentary lull before the next skirmish began.

Declan had fired a warning shot across her bow. He wanted the Brookfield Building and intended to complicate her life until he got it. And right now he had his sights set on destroying her relationship with Chase.

Which was why she intended to take full advantage of what time she had left with Chase, before he discovered what destruction she'd brought into his life.

Teagan launched herself at him as soon as he'd parked and opened the passenger door for her. Spinning, stumbling, kissing and tearing each other's clothes off, they made their way through his kitchen and upstairs to his bedroom. Naked and smiling, she fell onto the bed and watched with heady anticipation as he slid on a condom before coming for her.

He pounced on her, rolling them both across the mattress until he lay on his back and she straddled him. They came together in a practiced surge, Chase filling her in a powerful stroke that ripped a whimper from her. She bit down hard on her lower lip and rocked against him, loving the feeling of him inside her. His strong hands kneaded her breasts, driving her wild, while the friction of his plunging thrusts pulled at her clit. Teagan twisted her hips, grinding hard against him and climaxed fast.

With each wave of pleasure rolling into the next, she had no chance to catch her breath as Chase flipped her over, lifted her onto all fours and pushed inside her once more. With her first orgasm still rumbling through her, she dropped her head and savored the way his smooth, powerful thrusts started to build her hunger all over again.

When his teeth sank into her shoulder, claiming her in a wild, primal way, she came again and came hard. Yet, he still didn't follow her. Instead, he pulled her close, stilling all movement as he plied her buzzing ears with endearments and coaxing words. While her breathing slowed, he repositioned them on their sides. With his clever fingers, he drew soothing circles on her belly, making her tremble. His nose drifted into her hair where he hummed in delight. She smiled as his lips deposited tender kisses along her neck and at last, he began to move again inside her once more. This time his strokes were languid and tender, as if she was the most precious thing in his life.

Her last orgasm snatched her up in a different sort of wonder. Deeper and longer than the first two, rolling thunder rather than a blinding lightning flash. She savored the exhilaration of Chase's hoarse shout and the buck of his body as he came moments later. She clenched her inner muscles, determined to hold on to him as long as possible, as if by staying intimately linked she could keep the rest of the world at bay.

As her pulse slowed and her breathing became regular once more, Teagan floated in Chase's arms, all too aware that she was falling for this man. In moments like these she could pretend that they could become something that would last. It wasn't just great sexual chemistry. It was caring and camaraderie. She didn't just hunger for Chase's glorious form—she wanted to know everything that made him tick.

Turning and burying her face into the crook of his neck, Teagan savored the lethargic contentment that filled her. Yet it was hard to ignore the buzzing anxiety that tightened her chest and shortened her breath.

"It was fun listening to your mother tell stories about you and Nola growing up," she murmured, determined to focus on this precious moment and not dwell on potential future disasters. "You obviously had a happy childhood." Wistfulness tinted her tone. "No wonder you get along with her so well."

"I imagine it was different for you?"

"I can't remember a time when any of us were allowed to play as children. My parents always pitted us against each other. They lavished on my brother Aiden all the praise and attention the firstborn and male heir could possibly ever want or need. It made him entitled and lazy. Meanwhile, Sienna was mostly ignored. That may be what enabled her to turn out so nice."

"And you?" Chase prompted.

"I've always had issues surrounding being adopted." She continued to be astonished by how easily she shared her vulnerabilities with Chase. All the fears she kept hidden from family and friends seemed to roll off her tongue beneath his somber attentiveness. Despite knowing that he'd agreed to keep an eye on her for Ethan, she never worried that whatever she told him would come back to harm her. Trusting someone with her darkest secrets was novel for her, and yet because it was Chase, it wasn't at all scary.

"What sort of issues?"

"Always feeling like an outsider in my own family. It was as if a part of me was missing. My mother died shortly after I was born. My father wasn't in the picture. There was always this feeling that I wasn't wanted."

"The fact that you were adopted by the Burns family indicates that's not true."

"I was a beautiful child." She shrugged at the flare of amusement in his eyes. "It's not vanity. It's a fact. I know that because my mother often pointed out it was why she chose me to adopt. Sienna's a year older and when it became apparent that she wasn't the prettiest of children, my mother decided to get herself a toy she could dress up and show off to all her society friends."

Chase slipped his fingers through hers, the soothing gesture giving her the courage she needed to go on. "I imagine that hurt."

"Until I was nine, I didn't know any better. And then came the day when I overheard two women laughing about how much it embarrassed my mother to have produced such a plain daughter and how she'd only adopted me because I was pretty."

"Ethan mentioned your sister isn't close to your parents. Did she know how your mother felt?"

"Until I'd overheard those women, I never paid much attention to how Sienna looked. She was just my older sister who entertained me by drawing pictures and telling me stories. She's a really talented artist. Not that she would acknowledge it. I'm pretty sure she hasn't picked up a sketch pad or a brush since graduating college."

"Why not?"

"Our mother badgered the confidence right out of her. In our family, if you can't do something perfectly, then you shouldn't bother to do it at all."

"All of this sounds really harsh."

"By most people's standards it is, but the Burns family is like nothing you've ever seen. The smallest misstep can haunt you for a long time."

"So you developed a tough skin."

"I imagine that's not particularly attractive to you." She took his hand and guided his fingertips to her shoulder, smiling as he grazed her soft skin with his gentle touch.

"If you think I'm not attracted to you," Chase said,

dipping his head to kiss his way from her lips to her ear, "then you've not been paying attention."

"Oh, there's a big difference between this—" she gestured to her body and face "—and all that's ugly and broken inside."

"Have you forgotten what I do for a living?" His eyes glowed as he captured her gaze and held it. "Ugly and broken don't scare me."

Far from making her feel better, Teagan felt panic rising at his words. "You make ugly and broken things beautiful. Is that what you intend to do to me? To take everything that's wrong with me and fix it?"

Chase frowned. "That's not what I meant. The unique combination of perfection and flaws makes you special. I don't want to change you or fix you."

His earnest expression sent a ripple of pure pleasure dancing along her spine. It would be so easy to fall in love with this man. He seemed to know exactly what she needed to hear. Giving in to the strong feelings he evoked could place her on a tight rope without a safety net to save her if she fell.

"Not even a little?" she teased, cradling his face in her palms, her entire body surging with blinding joy at the way he was looking at her. "Admit it, you'd like it if I wasn't so selfish or prone to scheming."

"Maybe you're selfish and scheming because you've never had anyone taking care of you before."

"Damn," she muttered, unsure she deserved to be this happy. "You really are perfect."

After scrutinizing her expression for a long moment, no doubt trying to decide if she was bantering with him in an effort to dodge strong feelings, Chase rolled her beneath him and seized her lips in a hard kiss. Her heartbreak vanished in a furious explosion of desire. Teagan clung to him, worshipping the strong arms that held her and the gentle hands that caressed her skin. But before she went up in flames, Chase ended the kiss.

"No one who knows me would say I'm perfect," he told her, his lips moving across her eyelids and down her nose.

A sob caught in her throat at his tenderness. Rather than argue with him, Teagan decided to proceed a little farther along the treacherous path she'd set herself on.

"Okay, so I'll amend what I said." She summoned a deep breath and let it out on a shaky exhale. "You are perfect for me."

"Where are we going for dinner?" Teagan asked, taking in their surroundings as Chase left the downtown area and drove them fifteen minutes north to the "Neck" of the Charleston Peninsula.

"Bennett's Pub."

She glanced over her shoulder at the road behind them. "Isn't that downtown?"

"It is."

As the SUV passed through the white columns with their stately wrought iron gates, Teagan's attention sharpened.

"You brought me to a cemetery?" Her gaze moved across the numerous tombstones, both elaborate slabs of granite or carved sculptures and the more modest headstones that marked the passing of loved ones.

He nodded. "Magnolia Cemetery, where some of Charleston's most notable have been buried since 1850. It was created on the site of Magnolia Plantation after health concerns prohibited burials in the lower city."

He paused and glanced at her, seeing the tension building in her. "I thought you might be interested in seeing where some of your family are buried."

One golden eyebrow rose. "If this is supposed to get me hot, you need to rethink your seduction technique."

Although her words and tone were meant to be flippant, Chase heard a quiet echo of distress. Teagan's walls might be a mile thick, but they were pitted with holes. Between what she'd told him and what he'd gleaned from Ethan about Teagan's adoptive parents, a clear picture had formed in his mind of what her childhood had been like. Samuel and Anna Burns appeared incapable of bolstering the self-esteem of either daughter even as they lavished praise on their eldest son.

Both Burns sisters had grown into wary adults with significant trust issues. In the case of Sienna, she'd been swept off her feet by the magic of Charleston and Ethan's determined pursuit. Although the couple had gone through a rough patch thanks to Teagan's meddling, it hadn't taken Ethan long to realize he'd made a huge mistake letting her go back to New York without the air cleared between them. Chase had seen his charming best friend date all sorts of women, but not one of them had captured his heart like the down-to-earth art curator.

"I mean, sure, some women are turned on by graveyards." Teagan kept up her banter when Chase didn't immediately respond. "I'm not one of them."

He knew she was trying to bait him into playing her games, but he'd been around her long enough to recognize that her flippant, one-sided conversation masked confusion and anxiety. Interesting. What was worrying Teagan? He couldn't imagine her being afraid. Although the cemetery was a favorite spot for nightly ghost tours, in the afternoon, with sunlight filtering through the live oaks, the mood was tranquil and sacred.

"Over there is the special section reserved for Confederate soldiers killed during the Civil War," Chase declared, pointing to the neat rows of headstones.

Teagan sat in silence as he parked the car and shut off the engine. He took a moment to admire her beautiful profile as her gaze swept the final resting place of so many of Charleston's old families.

"Are you okay?" he asked, suddenly concerned by her fixed expression.

"Of course." She stopped picking at the fabric of her wide-leg pants and fluffed her long hair. "When am I not okay?"

"Never," he lied, reluctant to shatter her illusion of strength.

"Damned straight."

While Teagan was getting better at showing vulnerability, she preferred to pick her moments rather than have them thrust upon her. He was fast learning that while she enjoyed delivering surprises, she wasn't keen to be on the receiving end of them.

"Ready to meet your grandmother?" Chase asked, opening his car door. Without waiting for her reply, he circled the vehicle and opened her door. One glance at her face told him she was a million miles away. He held out his left hand to her while gesturing with his right. "She and the rest of your family are over there."

For several heartbeats Teagan stared at his hand while birds chattered in the tree branches above them. "What if she doesn't like me?"

His chest tightened at both the question and her lost-child voice. "Impossible."

"I can't believe I'm saying this," Teagan responded in aggrieved tones, "but you're right."

Tossing her golden mane, she set her palm against his and shifted her weight until one expensively clad foot reached the ground. Chase's pulse jumped at the warm glide of her fingers against his skin. Every time his body came into contact with hers, no matter how fleeting or inadvertent, it was like touching a live wire.

The strength of her effect on him should worry Chase more than it did. Ethan trusted him to keep his head around this woman. Disappointing those closest to him went against everything he believed in. Letting his hormones get the better of him was risky. Chase had made Ethan a promise and falling for Teagan jeopardized that.

And then there was the low hum of agitation that had gripped him since she'd returned from New York. Something was off. He would just have to work harder to keep his emotions in check while he figured out what was going on with Teagan.

"I think you'll find out I'm right about most things," Chase responded, knowing it would annoy Teagan. Focusing on her irritation would strengthen her.

"That's something we have in common," she said.

"It's like two immovable objects meeting. One of us will have to give."

Teagan shot him a sly grin. "Or we might just come to rest against each other, forever locked in a give-and-take."

Chase's gut tightened the way it did during a match when he realized he faced a more skilled opponent.

When it came to flirting, Teagan would always have the upper hand. He shifted his grip on her hand and wove their fingers together. She drew closer to his side and settled her head against his shoulder.

The wind whispered through the ancient live oaks as they strolled across the neatly trimmed grass. The hushed peacefulness of the cemetery wove a spell around both of them. At last, they reached the cluster of graves where the most of the Watts family had been laid to rest during the last century and a half.

"This is my family," she murmured, her gaze scanning the names and dates of her ancestors. Her grip on his hand tightened. "There are so many of them."

"George Watts came to South Carolina in 1792 and bought a plantation an hour north of the city. Shortly before the Civil War, the family moved to Charleston and founded Watts Shipping."

"You know so much more about my family than I do."

"Aside from the fact that our families have been friends for years, I'm in the restoration business. I know a lot about the history of Charleston."

Teagan let go of his hand and moved toward a headstone. "This is my grandmother." Her hushed voice barely carried the short distance between them. "Delilah Ann Bennett Watts."

"Descended from one of Charleston's older families."

"She died so young."

"The same year Ava left," Chase confirmed. "Your aunt Lenora insists her mom died of a broken heart, but it was really the cancer that took her."

"And Grady never remarried."

Chase shook his head. "He adored her. No other woman could compare. As many found out."

"It must've been hard for him to lose her so young."

"From what I've heard he was never quite the same after losing his wife and daughter in such a short span of time." Chase couldn't imagine the strength it must have taken for Grady to survive a double blow like that. "I think what kept him going was his determination to bring Ava home." He nodded toward one of the newer grave markers.

Teagan crossed to it and gasped. "It's my mom."

"I told you Grady was determined to bring her home. They found your mom buried on Hart Island in New York and brought her body back here."

"All these years she was here and I never knew." Teagan shook her head. "Wow."

Chase noticed the quiver in the hand he held. He glanced over and saw the sheen of tears in her eyes and the wobble of her lower lip before she caught it between even white teeth.

"You must think I'm ridiculous," Teagan declared with a weak chuckle, dashing the back of her free hand across her cheek. "I mean why should I get all upset? All my life I've known my mother was dead."

Chase's heart gave a sympathetic lurch. "I imagine it's a relief to know she's here."

"I wonder why no one told me she was here."

"You haven't been in Charleston that long. I'm sure someone would've gotten around to it."

"They might have if I hadn't screwed up my relationship with them." Self-reproach consumed her voice.

"Hey." Chase turned her to face him. "Nothing has happened that can't be fixed."

For a second, he thought his words might've penetrated the protective shell she'd built around herself.

"I've been trying, but no one wants to give me a chance to make things better." Brittle and dismissive, she spoke from a deep well of pain and frustration. "Oh, what am I even doing? I don't fix things. I break them. Isn't that why Ethan told you to keep an eye on me? To make sure I don't damage anyone else?"

"In the beginning, sure—"

"And now? You're with me because you think I've changed? Well, I haven't. I'm still the untrustworthy schemer I've always been. So, you'd better watch out or you'll get hurt, too." Teagan turned her back on her family's graves.

Her vehemence drove a spike of ice into his chest. Was she still scheming? Since returning from New York, she'd seemed troubled, but he'd brushed aside his worries with excuses about things going on with her businesses. But just now what she'd said left him thinking of a wounded animal snapping at anyone who reached out to help. Had something happened in New York that left her feeling desperate? Or was this just another facet of Teagan's personality that he'd not yet glimpsed?

Before Chase could settle on a reason for her outburst, Teagan was striding toward his SUV. He rubbed the back of his shoulder, digging his fingertips into the knots in his muscles, convinced the persistent tension hadn't been there before Teagan had entered his life.

Why was she so damned determined to present the ugliest version of herself? Did she really believe that if she actively made people dislike her, she wouldn't get hurt? As defense mechanisms went, it made no sense.

Didn't she realize the tactic's long-term disadvantages? If she never let anyone believe in her, how would she ever be truly happy?

Nine

Silence filled Chase's SUV as he drove them back to downtown Charleston. Although she was ashamed of her outburst and wanted to apologize, she hadn't yet come up with a reasonable explanation for her agitation. She really should tell him about her run-ins with Declan and the certainty that the Calloway house was on the verge of slipping through their hands. But every time she opened her mouth to explain how Declan was using Calloway to pressure her into selling the Brookfield Building, she imagined Chase's disgust and chickened out.

Once he heard the story, Chase was sure to hate her and she couldn't bear that. Nor would telling him stop the inevitable. She could only stay silent, hope Rufus Calloway believed in her vision for the property, and in the meantime, savor whatever time she had left with Chase. And that started with dinner tonight.

Bennett's Pub was a popular place because of its awesome patio. At night, strings of lights crisscrossed overhead, lighting the space and providing a festive ambience. Teagan had enjoyed several wonderful visits with her cousins and experienced a rush of melancholy as she and Chase made their way through the crowd.

With his ability to see over the heads of most of the patrons, he must've spied an open table, because he nudged her left. After another ten feet, Teagan came to an abrupt stop as she spied the couple in front of her.

Her throat closed up as she scanned her sister's stiff expression and Ethan's warning glare, before shooting a bewildered glance over her shoulder at Chase. His expression seemed to say, *You aren't the only one who can manipulate a situation.* Her heart pounded with joy and terror. What if Sienna refused to talk to her?

"This isn't an ambush," Teagan rushed to tell her sister. "I had no idea you'd be here."

"I know."

Old Sienna would've lowered her head, dropped her gaze and looked miserable. New Sienna had the benefit of a solid masculine presence at her side, a man who adored her and would cut down anyone who considered harming a single hair on her head.

"So, what do you want to do?" Teagan asked her sister. "Shall we parlay or retreat?"

Sienna sighed before saying, "Let's grab a glass of wine and talk." She indicated two empty stools at the bar. "Just us two," she added as Ethan stood to accompany them.

"Are you sure that's okay?" Ethan asked, shooting Teagan a suspicious glare.

"Sure." Sienna offered him a look brimming with

affection and appreciation. "Why don't you and Chase grab a drink? I'll be okay."

"Text if you need me."

The sisters made their way through the busy bar and snagged the barstools. After ordering two glasses of white wine, Teagan said, "I would've thought he'd know by now you can handle me."

"He does." A private smile curved on Sienna's lips as the bartender set the drinks before them. "He just wanted you to know that he has my back."

"I'm glad."

Sienna looked surprised at her sister's admission. "Really? Since when?"

"Since the day you went back to New York and left me alone in Charleston." Teagan snagged her sister's left hand and pulled it close so she could admire the diamond on her ring finger. "Nice. I'll say this much, the man has good taste. Congratulations."

"You don't think it's too fast?" The couple had known each other for less than two months and Sienna wasn't one to make major life decisions without weighing everything carefully. Yet, the pair had enjoyed an instant attraction and despite Teagan's scheming, they'd grown close during Ethan's journey to find his birth mother.

"Do you?" Teagan countered.

"No." A wide grin bloomed. "I can't wait to marry him."

"Have you set a date?"

"October, I think."

"That soon?"

"We don't want a huge wedding so there won't be a lot to prepare."

While Teagan wondered if Sienna would invite her, silence stretched, filling the space between the sisters while enthusiastic conversations buzzed around them.

"Look," Teagan began, hoping she was coming across as sincere. "I'm sorry about what I did to you and Ethan."

When Sienna spoke, her voice held remembered anguish. "I almost lost him because of it."

"I didn't know how serious it had gotten between you, and even if I had, I might not have stopped." Teagan dug deep to find the courage she needed to keep going. "I know it's not a good excuse, but some things that happened in New York this past year combined with my anxiety about being accepted by my Charleston family and made me unreasonable and irresponsible."

"What happened in New York?"

"I didn't tell you what Dad said to me when I told him I wanted to run Burns Properties. He said I had three strikes against me. I was not the oldest, I was a woman and I was not his biological child."

"Oh, Teagan."

"Being adopted has always bothered me, but that was a hit I didn't see coming." Teagan's throat tightened. "I guess when it comes down to it, Aiden was the only one of us both our parents wanted."

"Well, they're welcome to him," Sienna retorted in a rare show of bitterness. "Dad was crazy not to let you take over the business. Our brother will mismanage the portfolio into bankruptcy."

This was the most connected Teagan had felt with Sienna since they were teenagers. She regretted getting caught up in New York's cutthroat society and losing her sister in the process.

"So, you and Chase," Sienna murmured, doing a poor job of muffling her keen curiosity.

Teagan shook her head. "It's not like that." She refrained from adding that Ethan had asked Chase to keep an eye on her. It might sound as if she resented her cousin, when in fact, he'd done her a huge favor.

"Really? That's not the impression Chase gave Ethan."

Sienna's words jolted Teagan to her toes. "What did Chase say?"

"It's not so much what he said, but the fact that Chase talks about you constantly."

"We're collaborating on a house I want to restore." Teagan refused to give in to disappointment.

"So all those dinners together haven't led to anything more?"

A flush broke out on Teagan's skin, but she just shook her head.

"Oh, that's too bad." Sienna actually looked disappointed, as if she was wishing for all the best things to come to Teagan. As if the sisters hadn't exchanged painful verbal spears the last time they'd been together.

"Whatever." Teagan waved her hand. "He's made it perfectly clear that I'm not his type. And he wants to keep things professional between us." While that was no longer true, Teagan wasn't sure what Chase was looking for from her.

"You know," Sienna said, smiling warmly at Teagan, "I think coming to Charleston has been good for both of us."

"Maybe for you. You fell in love with the man of your

dreams. Meanwhile, I've alienated my long-lost family and pretty much everyone wishes I'd go back to New York."

"That's not true. You just need to be patient and it will all work out." That Sienna continued to support Teagan, despite the harm she'd done, demonstrated what a wonderful person her sister was. "But what I meant about you coming to Charleston is that you seem different now. In New York you had all this frenetic energy that needed an outlet. Your friends were always trying to outdo each other and nothing you achieved satisfied you." Sienna paused and scrutinized Teagan. "From what I hear you seem at peace these days."

Teagan's stomach muscles clenched at the idea that her family was discussing her. But what did she expect?

"What might've worked in New York backfired brilliantly here. I didn't understand how a tight-knit family would rally and support each other. I could've been part of the exact sort of family dynamic I've longed for, but I didn't trust that they'd accept me." Teagan clenched her teeth as misery swelled. "And now everyone hates me."

"They don't hate you."

"Distrust, then." Teagan took a big gulp of wine. "It was stupid of me to think I deserved to run Watts Shipping someday because I was a blood relative and Ethan was adopted. Stupid and callous considering how much it hurt when that was Father's rationale for giving Burns Properties to Aiden."

"Oh, Teagan, it'll all work out. You'll see."

"I don't think I'll be sticking around that long."

Sienna studied her. "You're leaving?"

"As people keep pointing out, my entire life is in

New York. I have three successful businesses there that I've been neglecting while chasing an impossible dream down here."

"Is it really impossible?"

"I came down here hoping to become part of a family," Teagan choked out, hating the way her throat tightened as anguish filled her. "Instead, I feel like an outsider."

"That's because you haven't let them in. All they've seen of you is the face you present to the world." Sienna reached out and covered her sister's hand with her own.

A gentle squeeze nearly shattered Teagan's heart. Lately, her emotional stability was as robust as a soap bubble. She was constantly on the verge of being torn apart from within.

"Are you two doing okay?" Chase's deep masculine voice spoke from behind her.

"We're fine," Sienna answered while Teagan sucked in a steadying breath.

His clean scent enveloped her like a warm blanket on a chilly morning, but she resisted the comfort of it and kept her spine ramrod-straight. The temptation to lean back against his solid strength was almost more than she could withstand, but she shouldn't get accustomed to relying on him that way. His sleeve brushed against her bare arm as he signaled to the bartender and her pulse stuttered at the glancing contact.

"Should we grab a table and have dinner?" Ethan asked, the offer indicating he'd put aside his earlier hostility—at least for the moment.

"Thanks, but I think I need to pass," Teagan said, desperate for the space to contend with her rioting emotions. "I'm suddenly not feeling well."

All three of them stared at her in concern, but it was Chase's keen gaze that pierced her.

His palm settled, warm and reassuring, into the small of her back. "I'll take you home."

"No," she insisted, the tightness in her throat making her voice hoarse. "You should stay and catch up. You and Sienna should get to know each other. I'll order a ride." Teagan glanced from Chase's unwavering care to her sister's confusion. "I'll be okay. I'm really glad we had a chance to clear the air a bit."

Sienna wore a slight frown as she nodded. "Of course."

"Maybe now you'll stop ignoring my texts?"

"I'm sorry. Of course, I will. I just needed some time."

"I understand." Teagan turned to Ethan. "I'm really happy for you two."

"Thanks."

If she thought Chase would let her walk out on her own, Teagan was doomed to be disappointed. As she made her way through the bar area toward the front entrance, he trailed after her. Once they stood outside, Teagan turned to him.

"You should go back inside. I'm okay." Desperate to escape before she dissolved into tears, Teagan keyed the rideshare app on her phone.

"Are you upset that I didn't tell you we were meeting up with your sister?"

Teagan desperately looked for the nearest available car. It was a few minutes away. She booked it and turned her attention to Chase.

"I'm actually glad that I didn't have a chance to prepare anything to say. I think it went better because I spoke from the heart." She tipped her head back and stared up into his face. "Things are better between us, so thank you."

"Then why are you leaving?"

Seeing Sienna and Ethan together had awakened Teagan to the emotional intimacy she longed to build with Chase. Despite the fantastic sex, mutual passion for historic buildings and his support as she'd laid bare her painful past, complete trust remained elusive.

He'd noticed that she'd been jittery since meeting Declan in New York. She longed to share her problems with him and work together to find a solution, but feared he'd turn on her once she warned him that at any second the Calloway house could be yanked away. Once she told him why Declan had gone after the house and how he planned to demolish it as punishment, Chase would regret ever meeting her. Nor could she stay silent and hope that Declan wouldn't contact Chase to explain exactly who was responsible for his family's loss.

"I'm really not feeling well." It was true, although her symptoms were emotional rather than physical. "And you should get to know my sister. Given how close you and Ethan are, she's going to be a big part of your life going forward."

"I guess that means by extension you will, too." He cupped her cheek in his large palm and held her mesmerized with no effort at all.

"It's hard for me to say what the future will bring." The lie was acid, eating away at their connection. She saw quite clearly what was in store for her and the anticipation of pain wrenched at her.

"What does that mean?"

"It's just that ever since I went to New York, I've

realized how hard it's going to be to extricate myself from my life there. I have businesses to run and my friends..."

"I thought you were planning on staying in Charleston." He looked confused, hurt, unsettled. "What happened to making your mark on the city and reconciling with your family?"

"As I said, I'll have to see how the situation plays out. I came here originally to connect with them and made a mess of things. Apologizing isn't getting me anywhere and I'm at a loss for what to do next." No matter what she did, what she'd done to hurt Ethan had kept her cousins from trusting her again. Teagan was beyond feeling lost and alone. "I'm no longer sure if staying makes sense."

"What about your plans to renovate a historic house?"

Chase was the only one anchoring her to Charleston at the moment and she needed some reassurance from him that he was the solid ground that would let her fight on.

"I really fell in love with the Calloway house and I don't know that I can move on to another property if I don't get it."

"Did you hear from Sawyer? Was your offer turned down?"

"Not yet." Teagan's heart contracted. She longed for Chase to sweep her into his arms and proclaim that he couldn't imagine his future without her, but that wasn't how he felt apparently. "I'm just bracing myself for a worst-case scenario."

Chase's eyes widened. "It sounds like you're giving up."

"I'm being sensible."

Luckily, Teagan's ride stopped at the curb before he could bombard her with more arguments. She pulled his hand away from her face and offered him a wan smile. Stepping toward the car, she jerked open the rear door and settled into the back seat.

"I'll call you tomorrow." Before he could reply, she shut the car door.

Her last glimpse of Chase tore at her heart. His stunned expression left her drowning in misery. He didn't know it yet, but she'd ruined everything for him. And when he found out that she'd chosen to hold on to her Manhattan building and put the Calloway house at risk, he'd never be able to forgive her.

Chase wound his way back through bar patrons and saw that Ethan and Sienna had secured a high-top table. His brain felt foggy as he angled toward them. What had happened to cause Teagan to bolt like that? He and Ethan had kept an eye on both women as they talked. The conversation had seemed to be progressing smoothly until the very end when Teagan had grown more and more agitated.

"Is she okay?" Sienna asked as Chase slid onto a stool at the table.

"I don't know." His instincts told him to protect Teagan, and he hated the way she'd withdrawn from him, taking whatever was bothering her onto her slim shoulders. "What were you two talking about there at the end?"

Ethan bristled as if Chase was accusing his fiancée of doing something wrong, but Chase ignored him. He wasn't interested in picking a fight, just gaining insight.

"She's really upset by how everyone continues to

give her the cold shoulder." Sienna shot a sideways look at Ethan. "I've seen her face a lot of setbacks but this is the first time she's ever seemed...helpless."

The description of Teagan's mental state kicked Chase in the gut. He glanced at his best friend. "Is there anything you can do to smooth things over? She's talking about heading back to New York. Possibly for good."

"She really got to you, didn't she?" Ethan's level tone wasn't quite flat enough to keep his opinion from showing.

"Yes." Chase wasn't going to make excuses or deny how he felt about her. "I've gotten to know her really well these last few weeks and she's more complicated than she seems."

Sienna's agreement reflected in her nod, easing some of Chase's angst. "She hides a lot of hurt behind her attention-seeking ways." Sienna grew pensive. "Usually, she lashes out when she feels threatened. This is the first time I've ever seen her run."

Run.

In his gut, Chase recognized that's exactly what Teagan was doing. Running. From Charleston. From her family. From him.

Chase's phone rang while they were ordering dinner. His pulse kicked up, hoping it was Teagan, and then slowed to a sluggish thump as Sawyer's name appeared on his screen. Disappointed, he shook his head at Sienna's hopeful expression and answered the call.

"Is Teagan with you?" Sawyer asked. "I've been trying to get ahold of her."

Hearing the tension in her voice, Chase didn't need

to be a mind reader to know that Teagan hadn't gotten the house.

"Rufus went with the other offer, didn't he?"

"Yes." Sawyer sounded as gutted as Chase felt. "Chase, I'm so sorry."

"Was it the guy from New York or did another offer come in?" As he asked, Chase noticed Ethan and Sienna exchanging worried glances.

"It was him. I gave Emmett a quick call and he said no other offers came in." Sawyer paused for a second and then said, "Chase, his offer was double the asking price. Why would anyone pay that much for that property?"

"I don't know." He closed his eyes and thought of what this was going to do to Teagan, to his mother. "I'll give Teagan a call and break the news."

"Thanks. Let her know I'll pull new listings for her when she's ready."

Chase hung up, thinking that there was no way Teagan was going to be ready to find a new property. He thought about how she'd spoken when they parted earlier. It was as if she'd had a premonition that bad news was coming and had been bracing herself to face it.

"What's going on?" Ethan asked.

"It's the Calloway house." Chase couldn't believe that after decades of waiting, the property had slipped away from them. "Teagan didn't get it."

"Oh, man." Ethan reached for Sienna's hand, a clear indication that these two were stronger as a couple than as individuals. "I'm really sorry. I know how important that house was to your mom."

"And to Teagan," Chase put in, swamped by the need to go to her and share in her disappointment.

"Did you say something about the other offer coming from someone in New York?" Sienna put in softly, her forehead puckered with a frown.

Chase nodded. "The guy paid double." He glanced at Ethan. "You know what the place looks like. Why would he do that?"

Again the couple across from him exchanged concerned looks. They obviously had something on their minds and Chase was in no mood to drag it out of them by degrees.

"Spill it. What do you two think is going on?"

"Declan Scott," Sienna said.

"The guy who messed with you two by sending all those anonymous texts?" Chase was dumbfounded. "That can't be right."

Sienna's pretty face tightened in anger. "This sounds exactly like something Declan would do to get back at Teagan."

"He wants something from her," Ethan murmured, his gaze turned inward.

Chase regarded him in annoyance, wondering why no one had thought to inform him of this threat until now. "Did he say what?"

Before Ethan could answer, Sienna inserted her own question. "When did you run into him?"

Ethan focused on Sienna. "Around the time you went back to New York. I found out he was staying down here and went to confront him. He said that…" Ethan swore viciously and looked pained. "Teagan refused to give him something he wanted and he intended to show her how that felt."

Sienna hissed through her teeth. "That sounds like Declan. I'm sure he wasn't happy that we found our way back to each other, and while I'm sure it amused him that her whole family turned their backs on her, he wouldn't let up until she came crawling."

The picture Sienna painted didn't sit well with Chase. The urge to fly to New York and punch the arrogant bastard in the face made him see red.

"What does she have that he wants?" Ethan asked, sighing in frustration as Sienna shook her head.

"When it comes to Declan, it could be any number of things."

Chase barely registered the exchange between Sienna and Ethan. Only two people knew the answer to why Declan had gone out of his way to hurt Teagan, and one of them was less than two miles away. His stool scraped against the concrete flooring as Chase pushed back from the table.

"I need to go talk to Teagan," he announced. "She needs to know what happened."

"Tell her to call me if she wants to talk," Sienna said.

With an abrupt nod, Chase headed for the exit. On the way to his vehicle, he tried Teagan's cell, but it rolled straight to voice mail. Either she was talking to Sawyer or her phone was turned off. His gut twisted as he replayed how he'd caught glimpses of anxiety and sadness in her since she'd returned from New York. Their limited time together hadn't enabled him to learn all her moods. In hindsight, he imagined a scenario where she'd run into Declan and their confrontation had rattled her.

Disappointment sat heavy on Chase's shoulders. Why hadn't she shared with him any of what was going on? It was possible she'd been utterly blindsided, but given the way Declan had taunted Ethan, the man enjoyed tormenting his foes. Teagan was accustomed to fighting her own battles and probably hadn't considered dragging him into the fray. He'd been under the impression that they had formed a partnership to restore the Calloway house, but obviously they weren't of like minds. What did that mean for what was happening between them romantically?

Earlier she'd made it sound as if she was ready to give up on making Charleston her home. Where did that leave him? Was their brief fling at an end? Despair flickered at the edge of his awareness. He wasn't prepared for her to go. There was so much more to explore between them.

Answers, he told himself as he pulled up to the Watts home. He needed answers.

At the door, when he asked after Teagan, Grady's housekeeper directed Chase to the back terrace overlooking the gardens. She looked startled when he stepped through the door and rose from the wicker sofa as he drew closer.

"What are you doing here?"

"Sawyer called me. She's been trying to get ahold of you."

"I lost the house." Calm. Matter-of-fact. Resigned.

"I'm sorry." He curved his fingers over her shoulders in an effort to comfort her, but she remained tense beneath his touch.

"Me, too." Teagan gave her shoulders a little shake and stepped back, dislodging his hands. "I know how much you want to restore the property for your mom."

"I was with Ethan and Sienna when Sawyer called. They thought that it might be Declan Scott who bought the house."

Teagan seemed to withdraw into herself at the news and wouldn't meet his gaze. Her voice was low and hoarse as she said, "It would be something he'd do."

Chase's gut twisted at her demeanor. He'd never seen Teagan look so completely miserable. Or…guilty?

"When Ethan spoke with him last month Declan indicated he was messing with you because you had something he wanted." He watched her closely as he relayed this. Again he sensed she wasn't surprised. "Is that true?"

"Yes."

So, did that mean the Calloway house had been lost because of some ridiculous war she was waging with Declan Scott? He held back his anger, determined to get the whole story before reacting.

"And you believe he's the one who put in the winning bid?"

"I know so."

Chase asked his next question with as much patience as he could muster. "How can you be so sure?"

"Because he told me. Threw it in my face actually. Damn him."

Her answer caught him on the temple, blindsiding him. "When?"

"While I was in New York."

She'd been acting different since returning to Charleston. At least now he understood why.

"Declan Scott bought the Calloway house." Chase couldn't wrap his head around any of it. "Why would he do that?"

"Because he knew I wanted it."

Ethan's words came back to him then. "Because you refuse to give him something he wants and he intends to show you how that feels?" Chase watched her reaction, growing ever more disturbed at the way her face hardened into a grim mask of resolve. "What does he want?"

"It's always something with him." Teagan waved her hand dismissively.

"What sort of something?"

"Suffice it to say that he and I have been engaged in an ongoing feud for a decade, and when things don't go his way, he plays dirty."

Chase recognized that Teagan hadn't actually answered his question and suspicion flared. The way she held her cards close was a clear warning. He wasn't hearing the entire story.

"So, the Calloway house has become a casualty of some sort of war you two are engaged in?"

"Yes."

"Is keeping the house away from you punishment enough?" Chase asked, wondering what sort of messed-up world she lived in where people hurt each other for sport. "Or does he have plans for it?"

"He won't sell it if that's what you're wondering." She grimaced, her gaze avoiding his. "It's only value to him is that he can use it as leverage against me."

"What sort of pressure can he put on you?" Chase took her by the upper arms and turned her to face him. Dread made his next words rougher than he intended. "Doesn't he realize that you can just go find a different property? Is he planning on buying up half of Charleston in his vendetta against you?"

Her body language indicated she was spoiling for a fight. This woman knew one way to handle setbacks—dig in and get dirty.

"He threatened to level it." As soon as the words were out, she looked stricken.

Chase's heart sank. What was wrong with Declan Scott that he would destroy a two-hundred-year-old treasure to get back at Teagan? And what had she done to deserve such treatment?

"He's going to tear down the house. My great-great-grandfather's home." Pain reverberated through his hushed voice.

No doubt seeing Chase's expression caused her temper to falter. "Oh, Chase," she said on a shaky breath. "I'm sorry. This is all my fault."

And it was. All of it. Despite all appearances, she'd learned nothing from the rift between her and her family. Now, another of her stupid games was on the verge of having real consequences.

Realizing he was still holding her, Chase whipped his hands away. Staring down at her beautiful face, he was consumed by self-loathing.

"On that, we both agree."

Ten

"How do we fix this?" Chase demanded, his gaze cold and merciless.

We. How do we *fix this?*

Had he used the plural pronoun deliberately? Did he still see her as a partner in their quest for the Calloway house? Or was he just a warrior going to battle to fight for something he loved and viewed her as a fellow soldier?

Whichever he meant, Teagan was dizzy with relief that he hadn't just stormed out of her life, abandoning her to the desolate void that had been her inner landscape before he'd shown her how magical life could be.

"I'm not sure we can." She breathed the last two words, scanning his granite expression, looking for some chink in his defenses she could cling to. "Declan has probably already wired the money to your cousin. There's no interrupting the sale at this point."

She wasn't going to sugarcoat the situation. He'd never believe her anyway.

Chase's eyes narrowed. "What about the thing you have that he wants?"

Teagan stopped breathing at the implication of what he was asking. Was she willing to give up something important to her to secure a different outcome? That was a damn fine question. She stood with one foot planted on two different destinies. She could keep the New York property and walk away from Charleston, her family and Chase, or she could surrender the Brookfield Building to Declan and start a new life in Charleston.

Having both was not an option.

If she screwed up in Charleston a second time, her family would ice her out forever and whatever she and Chase had begun to explore would be cut off. Even if she fixed the situation with the Calloway house, Chase might discover something else about her he couldn't live with and her biological family might always treat her as an outsider.

And if she kept the Midtown building away from Declan? She could return to New York, her pledge to her father intact, and resume her life as if these weeks in Charleston had never happened.

Only they had. And in meeting her blood relatives, and embarking on her relationship with Chase, she'd been altered. The process had been painful—a breaking of the defenses that had kept her safe from heartbreak. A resculpting of the protectiveness that enabled her to fight for her life.

Her old tricks no longer worked. Neither manipulation nor schemes brought her closer to what she truly wanted. Instead, she'd lost precious ground. Her future in Charleston had suffered a mortal wound. Yet, with the changes in her, returning to her old life in New York no longer seemed feasible.

Chase's grim stare succeeded in drawing an explanation out of her. "He wants a historic property."

He nodded, able to appreciate this much of what motivated her. "Why is it so important to him?"

"Declan is developing a block in Midtown, a tower that will bear his name and dominate the skyline." Teagan pondered the renderings she'd seen of the glass skyscraper and contemplated all the architectural gems that had once stood in its way. "The Brookfield Building occupies a tiny corner that he needs to complete the project."

To Teagan's surprise, sharing her story with Chase released some of her anxiety. Maybe she'd been wrong to keep her worries bottled up. The other things she'd shared with him had seemed to deepen their connection. Maybe going all in wouldn't end with rejection.

"If he was hoping to convince you to sell the building to him, it seems like a bad move to antagonize you."

"It's always like that between us." Teagan huffed a bitter laugh. "Declan doesn't charm when he can bully."

"So, Declan can't begin his project without you."

"It's not as if this is fun for me," she snapped, not liking the way Chase phrased his conclusion. He made it sound like she was deliberately blocking the property developer, as if messing with Declan was her agenda.

Chase didn't react to her vehemence, just kept marching forward with unrelenting wariness. "Is there a reason you don't want to sell him the property?"

"It's a historical building, built in 1895 in a Romanesque Revival style. The facade is ornamental red and white brick with a limestone colonnade base and cornice with spires. Not only is it striking, the building has a who's who of famous tenants."

Teagan couldn't help herself; she found the photos of the building on her phone. Like a proud mother showing off the child she adored, she extended the screen so Chase could see it. His gaze flicked from the building to her face and back down.

"I understand why you would hate to see it demolished."

Of course he'd understand. He'd devoted his life to preserving Charleston's history in its buildings and landmarks.

"Have you applied for landmark status?"

As if she hadn't thought of that. Stuffing down her indignation, Teagan said, "Back when Declan began buying up the buildings in the neighborhood. The Landmark Preservation Commission has eleven commissioners. Six are required to designate a landmark and Declan has a lot of *influence*." She put a particular emphasis on the last word and Chase nodded as he caught her inference.

"What about putting something in the contract that stipulates he has to incorporate the facade into the development?"

"He'd never go for it. The modern monstrosity he's erecting is Scott Tower, a tribute to his greatness. He's not going to want some old turn-of-the-century eyesore as its cornerstone."

"It sounds like you're in a bad spot."

She offered up a bland smile. "It's not the first one I've been in."

"What I don't understand is given how desperate he is to get the property, why did you buy it? He must've been in process with this project for years. Did you mean to get in his way?"

"I didn't purchase the property." Explaining how it had come to her would prompt more questions that she wasn't ready to answer.

"I don't understand."

"Someone gave it to me."

His eyebrows rose. "Why would they do that?"

"Because they weren't in a position to keep the property safe any longer and knew I was the best person to keep fighting Declan." That at least was the truth.

"Someone *gave* you a multi-million-dollar property." Chase shook his head in disgust. "What aren't you telling me?"

Not wanting to disappoint him, but unaccustomed to giving away any advantages in the midst of a skirmish, Teagan debated how much to tell Chase. It wasn't that she didn't trust him, but the reality was she'd only been sleeping with Chase for two weeks and she owed a lot to Edward Quinn, who'd not only mentored her, but had given her the encouragement lacking from the man who'd adopted and raised her. At the time she might not have known Edward was her father, but she'd loved him like a daughter.

Were she and Chase close enough that she could risk explaining their connection and trust that it would go no further? Because if Declan ever got wind that Edward was her biological father, he would use the information to hurt more people than just her.

"Obviously, it's something you aren't willing to share," Chase said when her silence stretched too long.

He stepped back from her, his body suddenly ram-rod-straight, his face devoid of emotion. His remoteness was unlike anything she'd seen from him before and it recalled every time she needed someone's support and they turned on her instead.

"You don't understand what Declan's like," Teagan said, her heart shrinking away from Chase's cold stare. "The lengths he'll go to win. He delights in playing dirty. In fact, I think he prefers it that way."

"So, what's your plan? How many more people are you going to let get hurt while you play his games?"

"That's not fair." Teagan dug her nails into her palms as her voice cracked. Helpless despair rolled over her. "Do you really think I'm doing this because I want to?"

"I really don't know." He surveyed her for several interminable seconds. "I guess there's nothing more to say. Obviously, you've made your decision."

"You make it sound like it's all cut-and-dried."

"Isn't it?" he countered. "You admit that you've known about his involvement since your trip to New York and didn't bother to warn me. Seems to me you've just chalked this up to a loss."

"You can't seriously think this is easy for me. You don't understand what the Brookfield Building means to me."

"How could I possibly when you won't tell me?" His voice cracked like a whip, but there was underlying pain beneath the frustration. "Did seven generations of your family live there? Do you have some sort of personal connection that would explain your stubborn need to hold on to it?" He paused, breathing hard while his cold gaze swept her. His next words came out on a lethal growl. "Or are you just determined to win?"

She felt as if he'd tried to run her over with his car. "Do you think I'm anything other than devastated by what Declan's been doing?" She paused for a brief moment, giving him space to answer. When he didn't, she rushed on. "I've been at war with him since we were in high school."

"Something about that must be working for you."

Teagan recognized that Chase was angry. With her. With the situation. But his criticism was a devastating wake-up call. The closeness she'd imagined between them was little more than the postcoital bliss of fantastic sex. Physical attraction wasn't trust and support.

"Did you ever believe that I gave up my scheming ways?" She scanned his expression and the last of her hope shattered at what she saw. "Why did you even bother to be with me if I was so abhorrent to you?"

"You didn't seem that way when we were together."

"Really?" Unshed tears burned her eyes. "Then how did I seem?"

"Warm and loving." His description shredded her heart.

"I guess I fooled you." She forced a bitter laugh, hating the shock that lashed across his face. "I mean, that's what you're thinking, isn't it?"

"I don't know what I'm thinking, really. I know what happened between you and Ethan. I know what you're willing to do to the people you love to get what you want. Am I supposed to believe that isn't who you are? That the woman I've held in my arms these past two weeks is the real you?"

Teagan sucked in a shaky breath. "So, you don't believe people can change." She threw herself into the fray already knowing her desperate campaign to change his mind had come too late. "That love can change people for the better?"

Even though he flinched at her use of the word *love*, she recognized that she'd been infatuated with him from the start. They'd had a lot of fun together. The sex had stirred her body and soul.

But Teagan had never known a deep, intimate bond or experienced a craving to make her partner happy. She was so accustomed to taking or receiving, believed she deserved to possess anything she fancied. Having never sacrificed for another's happiness, did she even know how?

"What are you saying?" He was a freight train of indignation. "That you've changed because of love?" His voice was harsh with dismay. "That you love me?"

"I'm not sure I know how." Avoiding any repeat of the word *love*, Teagan continued, "All I know is that since being with you I've been able to let my guard down and stop having to be invincible." She expelled her breath on a ragged little sigh. "It's exhausting trying to keep up the appearance of confidence while waiting for those around you to spot your weakness. I mean, look what happened with Declan and the Calloway property. He knew I wanted the house and how important it was to you and your family. That by snatching it away he harmed not only me, but your family. Destroying our relationship in the process made it almost too perfect."

Chase's eyes went wide as she brought the pieces together. "The instant you showed an interest in my family's home was the moment I lost everything."

"Not everything," she whispered, thinking of all the people who loved and supported him.

"No? How am I supposed to explain this to my mother? She liked you. Trusted you. Now, I have to inform her that the house she's been waiting all her life to save is on the brink of total destruction."

Teagan flinched away from his accusations, but what could she say to defend herself? She'd been so excited about the potential in the Calloway property, so thrilled to be working with a talented, passionate architect who got her vision. That her attraction for him had grown into a passionate connection with the potential for a truly deep and meaningful relationship had seemed so utterly perfect that she'd let her guard down.

This never would've happened if she'd been in New York. In familiar surroundings, where watching her back was as necessary as breathing, Declan never would've outmaneuvered her again. But becoming part of her Charleston family had distracted her. The Calloway house had excited her. And being with Chase had opened her heart.

One by one, Declan had ripped away what she loved. If anyone had lost everything, it was her.

After Chase finished throwing blame in her face, Teagan left him on the back terrace and fled inside. Abandoned to his anger and misery, he stood frozen, cursing himself for ever getting involved with Teagan Burns.

It wasn't like him to engage in problematic relationships either in business or his personal life. Consciously or subconsciously, he'd been holding out for the deep, committed love his parents had enjoyed. Which was why it made no sense how willing he'd been to tangle his future with Teagan, not knowing if she was looking for something that would last. The instant he'd agreed to show her the Calloway house, he'd started down a path to heartbreak. Instead of being drawn in by her excitement to team up for the restoration, he should've maintained his distance.

But he'd been caught off guard by the way she'd risked rejection when she'd opened up about her feelings for him—feelings she'd implied had grown into something powerful and transformative. *So you don't believe people can change? That love can change people for the better?* Chase shook his head to rid himself of the memory of her words even as he stared at the door through which Teagan had disappeared. Swept by a forceful yearning, he wanted to race after her and ask questions that had nothing to do with the trouble Declan Scott had stirred up.

Instead, Chase went in the opposite direction, down the circular iron staircase that led to the garden and along a crushed gravel path back to the front of the house. He spent the short drive to his mother's house wrestling with his churning emotions, but found no peace. As he pulled into his mother's driveway and shut off the SUV, Chase recognized that he was in no state to handle her grief. But how could he delay telling her? As it was, during his brief detour to talk to Teagan, someone might've called Maybelle and broken the news. Chase hoped that wasn't the case. His mother would need his support.

He'd forgotten it was her housekeeper's night off and stared at his mother in disconcerted silence when she answered the door. She wore a bright caftan and no makeup, but decades of a vigorous beauty routine left her looking far younger than her sixty-six years.

"Chase, what a surprise." She stepped back and ushered him inside. When he didn't move, she took a closer look at his face and frowned. "What's happened?"

Shaking free of his momentary paralysis, he stepped into the house and wrapped his arms around her. She made a startled noise and patted him on the back.

"You're scaring me."

"Sorry." He pushed her to arm's length. "I have something I need to tell you."

"It sounds serious."

She led the way to a cozy den at the back of the house where she retreated in the evenings to watch her favorite shows and work on her needle felting projects. The bookshelves were crammed with the figurine sets she'd completed throughout the years, including a collection of Disney figures her granddaughters adored.

Settling into her favorite chair, Maybelle clicked off the TV and gave him her full attention. "Go ahead."

Since his mother had always been a proponent of ripping off the Band-Aid, Chase wasted no time getting to it. "Teagan didn't get the Calloway house."

Maybelle sighed in disappointment. "I'm so sorry."

Her response confused him. "No, I'm the one who's sorry. This is all my fault."

Now it was his mother's turn to look puzzled. "How is it your fault?"

"If I'd discouraged Teagan instead of showing her all the plans I'd done that got her so excited about the house, she would've moved on to something different and maybe Sawyer could've found another buyer who would be interested in restoring the house."

From Maybelle's frown, his explanation hadn't made things any clearer. Chase explained to his mother all that he'd learned from Sienna, Ethan and Teagan that evening. She listened to him intently, saying nothing until he wound down and lapsed into silence.

"That poor girl."

Chase couldn't believe it. His mother was sympathizing with Teagan? She was the one who'd caused the entire mess.

"How can you say that?" he said, storming. "We lost the house because of her."

"Earlier, you said this was all your fault." His mother cocked her head and studied him. "Now, you're blaming Teagan. It seems to me that the true villain is the man who bought the house in order to force Teagan's hand."

"But it's Teagan who won't sell him the building he wants."

His mother's eyes narrowed. "And you think she should?"

"I…"

He knew exactly what he'd wanted to say. She should give up the building in New York and get the Calloway house back from Declan.

"I don't know if she wants to save this historic building or to beat Declan Scott. They have a long, antagonistic past." Chase could see his mother wasn't coming around to his way of thinking. "Look at the way she used her sister in a scheme to beat out Ethan as the future CEO of Watts Shipping. And three weeks ago Ethan asked me to keep an eye on her and make sure she didn't cause any more trouble."

Maybelle drummed her fingertips against the arm of her chair. "Do you consider me a good judge of character?"

"Of course," he growled, suspecting where she was going.

"And Sawyer, what about her?"

"I get it. You both like Teagan and I'm being too critical." Chase struggled for a way to make his mother understand. "But it's because of her that Declan Scott is poised to demolish the house that's been in your family for over a hundred years."

"Chase, it's just a house." His mother's soft words were probably the biggest shock he'd received on a day filled with bombshell revelations.

"A house you've wanted to save for decades."

She shook her head sadly. "Not at the cost of hurting anyone."

And that's when it hit him how badly he'd handled the situation with Teagan. Had he really prioritized a rundown house over the woman he'd made love to? Would she have shared her troubles if his doubts hadn't made him insensitive to her disappointment and fears? Maybe if he hadn't limited his emotional response to her and given her a glimpse into how he felt, she might've trusted him enough to explain why Declan Scott had been terrorizing her.

The vastness of his failure shocked Chase. "I really screwed up."

His mother picked up an oblong lump of pink wool and her felting needle. "I'm sorry to hear that."

Her disappointment made him feel worse than if she'd scolded him for a solid hour.

"I think after what happened she's going back to New York."

"You can change her mind."

His stupid, rebellious heart leaped with hope. Chase wrenched it under control. "I don't know if I should."

Maybelle stopped what she was doing and stared at her son. "Why ever not?"

Because it would require not just an apology, but a plea for her to stay. And she would want to know why—to know what was in his heart.

"All her friends are in New York," he said instead, the excuse sounding lame even to his ears. "She runs three businesses there. Do you really think she's going to give all that up?"

His mother's look seemed to say, *She would for you.* But her answer was much more practical. "Teagan has family here. She intends to do good things in Charleston."

"Her family won't speak to her."

"She has you."

"That's a big leap," he said, the words tasting like ash. "I've only known her a few weeks."

"I learned long ago not to believe a man's words, but to pay attention to his actions. No matter what you say, you've been behaving like a man who's falling in love."

Her words were a tornado axe kick straight at his jaw. Mind reeling, Chase automatically defended his position, forgetting that facing an opponent with his emotions engaged would only lead to defeat.

"We're so different," he argued. "She's not at all who I imagined spending the rest of my life with."

"Hmm," his mother muttered noncommittally, picking up a long strand of pale gold wool.

"Life with her would be a roller coaster ride."

Was he up for that? And what convinced him that she would remain interested in him long-term? But the thought of losing her filled him with dread. How could he survive not seeing her every day and making love to her every night? She was the first woman who'd ever annihilated his guard and warped his common sense. No wonder he had gone a little crazy.

Like it or not, he'd fallen in love with Teagan Burns. And he suspected it had happened the day she'd gamely joined his beginner martial arts class and learned how to stand, fall and strike alongside a group of five-year-olds.

"I have to fix this," Chase murmured.

"Yes, you do," Maybelle agreed without looking up, but as she focused all her attention on the blonde princess coming to life in her hands, his mother was smiling.

Eleven

After she left Chase on the back terrace, Teagan went straight to her room and locked herself in. Dry-eyed and miserable, she threw herself on the bed and stared at the ceiling while regret and self-loathing pummeled her spirit.

Was this the pain Sienna had experienced when Teagan's scheming had come to light and her sister had ended things with Ethan? Teagan pressed her palm against her aching chest and beat down the urge to cry. It wasn't in her nature to surrender to emotional distress. Usually, she swallowed the difficult feelings, came up with a new strategy and enacted some plan that would ensure she came out victorious.

But how could she win when the only man who'd ever truly made her happy was disgusted by the person she was? She had no one to blame but herself. It was one thing to control the narrative. She'd owned up to behaving in a way that had alienated her sister and her Charleston family. Maybe she hadn't demonstrated the proper amount of regret, but that didn't mean their hostility didn't hurt.

She hated exposing any sign of weakness. Letting anyone glimpse the anxiety and self-doubt beneath her sophisticated exterior meant dropping the armor that kept her safe. This meant no one really knew her. Not even the sister Teagan loved.

Sienna had witnessed how their mother's selfishness and their father's dismissal had affected Teagan, but she had her own issues with their parents. Maybe if Teagan had asked her sister for help, the two of them could've stood against their parents and become happier for the mutual support. Instead, Teagan had studied social strategies from her aloof, ambitious parents and sculpted herself into a titanium socialite with a Teflon coating.

After a mostly sleepless night, Teagan pulled out her phone and dialed Sienna's number. To her surprise and delight, her sister answered.

"I'm just calling to say I'm sorry for bailing last night," Teagan began. "And for what I did to you and Ethan. I know I already apologized and I meant it, but I didn't understand how much pain you were in when you left Charleston. As always, I was selfish and insensitive."

"It's okay." Sienna's voice was soothing and kind. "Chase told us what happened with the house. Why won't Declan stop messing with you?" Sienna's furious outburst nearly made Teagan smile. "What is wrong with him? Can't he just leave you alone?"

"He wants the Brookfield Building. It's the only property left standing in the way of his tower."

"What does that have to do with you?"

"I own it and he's been badgering me to sell it. If I don't, he's threatening to destroy everything and everyone I love in order to get it."

"So sell him the damned thing and be done with it."

"I can't." Teagan sucked in a deep breath. She was so accustomed to keeping things to herself that sharing her secrets was like having a tooth ripped out without Novocaine. "Edward Quinn left the building to me."

"He left it to you?" Sienna sounded both surprised and puzzled. "Why?"

"Because it was the first property he ever owned and it's an architectural gem. He trusted me to do the right thing with it."

"I get that, but Edward is gone and Brookfield is only a building."

Teagan hadn't told her sister about discovering her biological dad. Only Chase knew that much, and yet she hadn't been brave enough to share his identity. Nor had she explained to Chase her father's connection to the Brookfield Building and why Teagan was clinging to it. Suddenly Teagan was tired of keeping everything to herself. It was time to let someone all the way in. And who better than her sister?

"Edward was my father."

From the silence that followed the announcement, Sienna was having a hard time absorbing the news. "Your father?" she finally said. "Oh, Teagan…" Empathy filled her sister's strangled exclamation. "How long have you known?"

"Not until after he died. When he left me the building, he included a letter with the deed, telling me about the affair with my mother and asking me to keep our true relationship secret."

"Is that why he mentored you?"

"I think so. It would've been nice to know back then, but in the end, it didn't change my love for him. He was the one person who believed in me without reservation."

"That's not true. I've always been in your corner. Just because I don't approve of your tactics doesn't mean I'm not cheering you on to victory."

Gratitude flooded Teagan. "I appreciate that. Although I'm not sure I deserve it. I haven't always been the best sister to you."

"Not true. You were the only one who encouraged me to go to art school."

Teagan was surprised that her sister had appreciated such a small thing. On the other hand, given the way they'd been raised, even the tiniest bit of encouragement could go a long way.

"You're incredibly talented. It was the perfect place for you." And the experience had given Sienna the confidence she needed to become an art curator, a career she not only loved, but was also spectacularly good at.

"Have you explained to Chase about Declan and the Brookfield Building?" Sienna asked, getting back to the heart of Teagan's problem.

"Yes."

"And about the fact that you inherited it from your biological father?" Sienna blew out an impatient breath at Teagan's lack of a response. "You have to tell him."

"It won't change anything. Declan is still going to

tear down the Calloway house and Chase will never forgive me for putting his family in the line of fire."

"You can apologize to him," Sienna pointed out. "I'm sure he'll forgive you."

"I've already apologized." Teagan blew out a hopeless sigh. "He's too angry with me to listen to any of my excuses."

"Saving a building your father spent his life protecting is not an excuse. It's what Chase has been doing with the house that belonged to his mother's family. He'll understand your decision." Sienna paused to let her sister speak, but the lump in Teagan's throat prevented any words from breaking free. With a sigh, Sienna added, "You can't keep shutting everyone out and trying to handle things by yourself when you feel threatened."

"Not everyone." But even as the denial left her lips, Teagan recognized the truth in Sienna's statement. "Okay, so I suck at letting people in."

"You started by trusting me. Now, trust Chase."

"I think it's gone too far for that," Teagan said.

"I don't know Chase all that well, but from everything Ethan has said about him, family comes first. He'll understand you're honoring your father's final wishes."

"And what about his mother's wishes?" Teagan prompted, thinking back to Chase's comment about his mother's heartbreak. "It's been her lifelong dream to restore her family's house. Thanks to me it's going to be gone forever."

"That's Declan's fault. Not yours."

"It's two sides of the same coin."

"So, what do you plan to do?" Sienna asked. "I'm

sure you realize that as important as that building is to Declan, he's never going to stop until he gets it from you."

"I know." And her future looked lonely and bleak because of it. "I think I have to go back to New York. If I'm not here, hopefully Declan will stop messing with you all."

"But you and Chase…"

"That's over."

"I don't think so."

Teagan's heart fluttered. "What makes you say that?"

"Because I saw you two together and I recognize love when I see it."

As tempting as it was to accept her sister's opinion as gold, Teagan leaned toward skepticism. Sienna was newly in love, so of course she was optimistic that her sister had made her own romantic connection.

"He's not in love with me," Teagan murmured. "And he never will be. I'm just the woman who he's been sleeping with for a few weeks." She laughed bitterly to cover her anguish. "The one he agreed to keep an eye on for his best friend in case she caused more trouble." Teagan paused to let Sienna absorb that. "I'm pretty sure he's kicking himself for getting blindsided."

A sob mangled the last word. The tears she'd been struggling to hold back rushed up and spilled down her cheeks. For several seconds she couldn't breathe, couldn't talk and couldn't stop the panic spreading through her.

"I don't think you're giving him enough credit. He looks at you like you're the most amazing woman on the planet."

"That was before we found out about Declan buying the Calloway house."

Sienna was quiet for a long moment and then she said, "Ethan is going back to Savannah tomorrow. How about I stay in Charleston through the weekend? We can hang out and talk."

"I'd love that," Teagan declared gratefully, her voice a shaky mess. "You're always there for me. I hope you know how much I appreciate you."

"I do."

"I'm going to book us a suite at Hotel Bennett," Teagan said, overwhelmed with love for her sister. "They have an amazing spa there so we can pamper ourselves, eat room service, raid the minibar and talk. How does that sound?"

"Like the perfect weekend with my sister."

Teagan had never been so grateful to hear Sienna call her that. "I love you," she said, her spirit noticeably lighter since the phone call began. "I can't wait to hug you."

"I love you, too. Hang in there."

As much as she'd enjoyed reconnecting with her sister over the weekend, Teagan couldn't shake her misery over what had happened between her and Chase. It didn't help that Sienna was blissfully preoccupied with Ethan, planning a fairytale wedding and busy expanding her art curating business in the area. The sisters had grown closer than ever over the last two days and Teagan was determined to nurture their connection.

Teagan had spent her time away mulling her future plans and arrived at no clear direction. Although her heart longed to stay in Charleston, Teagan recognized that Grady was the only other person besides her sister that would encourage her to remain. As soon as she entered her grandfather's house, Teagan located Grady in his favorite spot in the living room and settled beside him. His fond smile made her throat contract. As excited as she'd been to meet all her Charleston relatives, Grady had touched her heart the most.

"Chase took me to Magnolia Cemetery," she told him. "I saw where both my grandmother and my mom are buried. Thank you for bringing her home. It makes me happy to know she's back where she belonged."

"She was never happy here." Grady sighed deeply. "But I couldn't leave her all alone in that New York graveyard."

"Everyone who knew her says she was a wild child. I guess the excitement of New York was a lure she couldn't resist."

"My daughter was headstrong and wouldn't listen to anyone. I worried about her in that big city all by herself. And it turns out I was right."

"I thought you might like to see this."

Teagan pulled out the other item her father had left her, an old photo of Edward and Ava taken in Central Park. They sat side by side on a blanket, beaming at the camera. From the date on the back of the photo, Teagan figured her mother had been about three months pregnant at the time. Whether Edward knew was unclear, but Teagan wanted to believe that when he'd found out, he'd been happy.

"This was my dad." She handed Grady the photo. "His name was Edward Quinn. He was an amazing mentor and taught me everything I know about New York real estate. I didn't know he was my dad until after he died when I received a letter from him and this picture." Teagan sucked in a shaky breath as her grandfather smoothed his fingertips across his daughter's beautiful smile. "He also left me a historic building. It's that particular property that's been causing a great deal of trouble for me and everyone around me."

While Grady listened intently, Teagan went on to explain about Declan and the anonymous texts he'd sent to Ethan about her, and how she'd created problems between Ethan and her sister in her quest to be accepted by the family. She explained about Chase and how Declan had bought his family's house and was planning to destroy it if Teagan didn't sell him the Brookfield Building.

"What should I do?" she asked as her tale wound to an end.

"I guess the question you first need to ask is what do you want?"

"I want to keep all of you safe and that means getting Declan off your backs."

Grady waved his hand, dismissing her words. "Don't worry about us. We Wattses have endured tougher opponents than Declan Scott. What will make you happy?"

"Getting back the Calloway house for Chase. I was so happy when I thought he and I were going to be able to restore his family's home together. Plus, I want to create a safe place for victims of domestic violence."

"But to do that you need to give up the legacy your father left you."

Teagan nodded. "How can I choose between them?"

"I guess it's the difference between holding on to the past or sacrificing for your future." Grady took her hand between both of his. "Tell me, if your father was here today, what would he tell you to do?"

Teagan laughed. "He'd tell me to get the Calloway house back and stick it to Declan in the process."

"Then, that's what you should do."

Seeing the mischief in her grandfather's eyes, Teagan's heart clenched. This was the acceptance she'd longed for—the support of someone willing to take her side even when she screwed up.

"Then, that's what I'll do." Teagan swallowed hard. "And when I come back to Charleston, I promise I'm going to find a way to make amends with everyone. I know I've made mistakes, but I'm not the same person I was when I came to Charleston. I hope I can show everyone that I've changed."

"I'm glad to hear you talking like that," came a deep masculine voice from the doorway leading to the hall.

Teagan turned to face Paul Watts and blinked as hot tears filled her eyes. "You are? I wish the rest of your family felt the same. After everything I did to Ethan, they're having a hard time forgiving me."

"I'll talk to them." Paul's somber green gaze flicked towards Grady. He studied his grandfather's expression for a long moment before returning his attention to her. "We spent too many years looking for you to give up on the relationship."

Paul's words filled Teagan with hope. As the eldest of the cousins, his opinion counted for a lot.

Clutching her grandfather's hand, Teagan swallowed the lump in her throat and whispered, "I'm really happy you feel that way. Thank you."

Twelve

A few days later Teagan strolled into Declan's office with the contract he'd presented to her some weeks earlier. The satisfaction in his smug smile made her blood boil. Although she and Ethan had spent the last few days brainstorming possible ways to outsmart Declan, nothing they'd come up with could save both historic buildings from being torn down.

In the end, Teagan accepted she could save either the Brookfield Building or the Calloway house. The choice stopped being complicated when she realized that choosing Chase's happiness took the sting out of failing her father. She'd ruined any hope of a future with Chase the instant she endangered his family's home, but she would delight in knowing that he would look out his window every morning and revel in the Calloway house being restored to its former glory. And maybe he'd think fondly of her and not regret their time together.

"I'm glad you've come to your senses," Declan said, watching her with predatory glee.

"You didn't give me much choice."

"What are you talking about? It's your choice to sell me the Brookfield Building in exchange for the Charleston property you want."

"Don't forget the other part of our deal. You promise to never contact me again."

Declan's grin grew positively vile. "You'll be bored without me around to challenge you."

"Challenge me?" Teagan scoffed. "Is that what you think you're doing? More like you've made it your life's work to ruin anything that makes me happy."

"I suppose you're talking about that derelict shack you want so badly to own?" The sarcastic twist to Declan's question broadcast just how little he thought of Teagan's version of happiness.

Teagan defensiveness flared. "It's going to be beautiful when I'm done restoring it."

"I imagine your boyfriend was pretty upset with you for losing it to me. Are you even together anymore?"

"No," she admitted, bitter defeat in her tone.

Declan snorted. "But you're hoping this grand gesture will win him back? Why are you bothering? Why waste your time on some small-town architect? I guarantee you'll be bored with him inside six months. New York is where it's at. With what I've offered you for the Brookfield, think of the empire you could start with that."

"I don't want an empire," Teagan replied, thinking about Chase and her dream of being accepted by her family and making a positive impact on Charleston. "I just want a place where I belong."

"You don't belong in that backwater town."

Teagan bristled at his scathing remark. "Charleston is a historical gem and it's where my roots are."

Declan arched his eyebrows, looking entirely bored, but there was avarice in the gaze he slid toward the envelope in her hand. "Did you sign the contract?"

"Yes."

Adrenaline surged, goading her pulse to greater speed as Teagan nodded. To an outsider it must've looked as if she was trading a diamond tiara for a necklace made of macaroni. But for her, the value of each wasn't in its market price, but its sentimental worth. To her. To Chase and his family.

As Declan reached out his hand for the envelope, raised voices came from outside in the hall. Declan paid the disruption no heed; his gaze remained fixed on the envelope. Teagan turned as the office door opened and Chase strode in.

She gaped at him. "What are you doing here?"

With her full attention riveted on the determined set of Chase's sculpted lips and the flash of concern in his eyes, she barely noticed Declan step forward and seize the envelope in her hand.

"Stopping you." Chase executed a swift martial-arts move that forced Declan to release the envelope with a grunt.

Teagan clutched the envelope to her chest. Her heart expanded at his rescue. Never before had anyone tried to save her—from herself or any of the battles she'd waged. She'd always fought unaided, schemed to balance the power inequity.

"Don't do this." Chase's expression was earnest as he stood before her, his hands clamping on to her forearms. "We can figure out another way."

"There's no need." With trembling fingers, Teagan reached out and cupped his cheek. She smiled into his blazing eyes and whispered, "Let me do this for you."

Chase turned his lips into her palm. The kiss shot a lightning flash of joy through her.

"You've already given me so much," he murmured. "I'm sorry I didn't believe in you before."

"It's okay." And it was. She could see that he believed in her now and that was all that mattered.

"But I *know* what the property means to you."

Despite his special emphasis on the word *know*, Teagan was certain he had no idea of her true attachment. She'd only shared the truth with Sienna and Grady. Both had promised to keep it secret, which meant that Chase had chosen to sacrifice something important to him and his family so she could be happy. Teagan never imagined her love for Chase could grow more powerful, but obviously she had a lot to learn. She smiled, imagining the infinite joy the future held for them.

"Not as much as you do," Teagan told him, before glancing toward Declan, who watched their exchange with disinterest. "We have a deal. I sell you the Brookfield Building in exchange for the Calloway property."

Declan's handsome face lit with triumph as he reached out for the envelope.

Teagan held it out of reach. Did Declan think that love had turned her into a fool? Before she gave him everything he wanted, Teagan intended to extract an important promise.

With Chase's muscular body offering her his strength,

his hands cupping her shoulders in a show of unity, she said, "And you agree to leave me—and everyone close to me—alone forever?"

Declan took in the towering sentinel behind her and sneered. "Out of sight. Out of mind."

"Good." She dropped the contract on his desk, then, reaching into her purse, she extracted her cell phone and sent a text. "I've wired what you paid for the Charleston house."

She leveled a stony stare at Declan until he summoned his assistant and arranged to pay her the amount agreed to in the contract they'd both signed. A few minutes later, another text appeared on her phone, confirming the transaction.

"You'll probably want these." Declan tossed a courier envelope her way. The metallic clink of keys sounded as the projectile came straight at her head.

Teagan was too stunned to duck and only Chase's sharp reflexes, honed by years of martial arts training, kept the sharp corner of the package from striking her cheek. She didn't need to hear Chase's incensed growl to recognize that his restraint was on its last thread.

"Let's get out of here." Teagan caught Chase's free hand and tugged him toward the exit. "We have a whole lot of celebrating to do."

In his eagerness to put distance between Teagan and Declan Scott, Chase set a blistering pace on the way to the elevator bank. Teagan's heels clicked a staccato rhythm as she kept up with Chase's stride. Despite his best efforts to convince her to not let Declan have the Brookfield Building, he'd failed her. Chase said nothing until they entered the empty car and the doors slid shut.

"Why did you do that?" he demanded. "Why did you sell Declan the building your father trusted you to keep safe?"

Teagan gazed at him in shock. "How did you know about my father?"

"Sienna told Ethan. He told me."

A disappointed sigh slipped past her tight lips. "She promised me she'd keep it a secret." But there were no secrets between Sienna and the man she adored, unlike those that had separated her and Chase.

"Why?" Chase arched an eyebrow. "Because you had this noble sacrifice planned and didn't want me to interfere?"

"It was all I had to bargain with," Teagan insisted. "And I didn't want you to think I was manipulating you into owing me something in return."

"But I don't understand. Why would you give it up?"

"To save the Calloway house."

Chase kicked himself for guilting her into the rash act. "You shouldn't have done that."

"Why not? It's important to your family and I would do anything in my power to see it saved."

"I'm sorry." The apology rumbled out of him, but Chase knew it wasn't enough. He owed her not just his gratitude, but his trust and admiration. "I said all the wrong things to you that night on the terrace."

"You were angry and disappointed."

"That's no excuse. I had no business taking it out on you. Especially not after I failed to create a safe space for you to confide what Declan was up to."

"I'm not good at asking for help."

"Because you've faced too much rejection when you have."

He'd listened to her stories but hadn't comprehended the impact on her behavior until he'd witnessed her actions firsthand. With the love and support his family and friends provided, he couldn't imagine her coping with difficulties alone.

"Are you going to be okay? Declan has the only thing your father ever gave you."

"It might seem that way, but while it's the only tangible thing I ever received from him, what matters to me is what I gained all those years he mentored me. Edward believed in me when my parents didn't. He taught me how to appreciate historic architecture and awakened my passion for preservation and restoration." Teagan smiled. "From him I learned how to fight for what I believed in and that it's okay not to get what you want if the people you love are happy."

Any response he might've made was halted as the elevator stopped, the doors opened and two men stepped into the car.

"Thank you for having my back today," she began softly, staring at the descending numbers. "How did you know where I'd be?"

"Paul tracked your phone."

Eyes flashing, Teagan stared at Chase. "He tracked—"

"I didn't want you facing him alone."

Before he could add anything more, the elevator doors opened, depositing them in the lobby. As they headed toward the exit, Chase tucked her hand into the crook of his arm, noting the icy chill in her fingers.

A black town car awaited them at the curb. Teagan drew Chase toward it. The driver opened the rear door and Teagan settled in with Chase beside her. While they waited for the driver to get behind the wheel, Chase handed her the shipping envelope Declan had tossed at her.

"Declan didn't seem too happy about letting you have this. Do you think he'll leave you alone going forward?"

Teagan withdrew the keys. "He might be a ruthless businessman, but he's never been one to go back on his word."

"Not even to take revenge?"

"Against me?" She cocked her head and studied him with raised eyebrows. "Whatever for? He got what he wanted."

Chase almost smiled as he pondered the surprise that awaited Declan.

"We're in your debt," he told her. "I'm in your debt."

Her lighthearted mood dimmed. "That's not why I did it. I don't want you to feel like you owe me. It was the right thing to do." She gave a self-deprecating laugh. "No one's ever accused me of doing the right thing before."

"That's not true." He thought about his long conversation with Sienna. Teagan might downplay the good she'd done, but a long list of people who'd once needed help owed her a lot. "We all misjudged you."

"No, I think you all judged me perfectly." Her expression tensed. "I am a self-absorbed know-it-all that runs roughshod over people."

"But you're more than that. You're quick to help people who need it. And you don't expect anything in return."

"So you'll be thinking fondly of me from here on out?" Beneath her radiant grin lurked candid vulnerability.

Chase put his arm around her and drew her close. He cupped her cheek and grazed his lips over hers. "I've been thinking fondly of you for a long time."

"Stop." She sagged against him, her breath puffing against his cheek. "Your Southern charm is showing and you know I'm quite susceptible to it." When he slanted his mouth along her jawline and down her neck, she groaned. "Keep that up and…"

"And what?" He nipped at the sensitive spot where her neck joined her shoulder.

Her fingers tunneled into his hair, drawing him closer. "I have a private plane waiting to take me back to Charleston," she purred. "Let's get on it and I'll show you."

"I like the sound of that, but before we do, let's take a little detour." He gave the driver the address for the Brookfield Building and noted Teagan's jolt of surprise.

A shadow passed over her expression. "Why are we going there?" She sounded both mystified and sad.

"I thought you'd like to get one more look at it."

"Before Declan tears it down?" A vigorous shake of her head betrayed how hard giving up the building had been. "No thanks."

"But I've never seen it in person and I'd like to, very much," Chase insisted. "It's important for me to appreciate what you gave up so that the Calloway property could live on."

"It wasn't the sacrifice you think," she said. "It wasn't just for you. I did it for us. I really want you and me to collaborate on restoring your family's home. I'd like for us to create a charitable foundation for the property so that it will be safe forever." She offered him a tremulous smile. "I think your mother would like that, don't you?"

"I can't let you do that," he told her, thinking of the hefty purchase price. "It's too much."

"Are you worried that I might ask for something in return?"

Her mischievous expression told him she was teasing, but it was hard to ignore the way his stomach muscles clenched. "Whatever you ask for, I would willingly give."

"That's a dangerous offer you've just made. I could ask you for all sorts of things you'd hate."

"I'll take that chance," he told her. "What's your fondest wish?"

"The chance for a fresh start." Her smile was like a sunrise. "With you."

Her words kicked him in the gut. "Teagan…"

"Being with you helps me be the best version of myself and I'm a little afraid to leave your shadow for fear that I'll regress and become someone you won't want to be with."

"I don't think that could ever be possible."

"Then why did you push me away?"

"Because the way you make me feel is so strong. I was afraid of it. Until you came along, my only passion was for historic restoration. And then you blew into my life with your sassy New York vibe and your knack for turning my world upside down and opened my heart to what I've been missing." He ran his knuckles across her flushed cheek. "I love you."

Her eyes shimmered with unshed tears. "I love you, too."

"I don't want to live another second of my life without you."

The town car came to a stop beside the building that

had mattered so much to Teagan and her father. Excitement sped through Chase as he drew Teagan from the car and stood beside her on the sidewalk, staring up at the building. The architect in him appreciated the ornamented red-and-white brickwork and limestone cornice bookended by twin spires at the corners, echoing the church spires across the street.

"It really is amazing," he murmured.

"Too bad Declan is going to tear it down." Despite the brave face she'd been wearing, Teagan's voice throbbed with despair.

"He will find that hard to do."

Chase reached into his inner coat pocket and drew out a rolled-up piece of paper. It was fastened with a bit of red silk ribbon for drama. Something sparkled in the middle of the bow and Teagan gazed in confusion from the scroll to Chase.

"What's this?"

With a smile, he unfastened the bow and held the paper in one hand, the glistening diamond ring in the other. "Which would you like to talk about first?"

"Why is it only during the big moments that your sense of humor appears?" She exhaled in a rush and pointed at the diamond ring.

Nodding in approval, Chase dropped to one knee before her. "Teagan Burns, my love, I want to restore properties and raise children with you for the rest of our lives. Will you marry me?"

"Oh, yes." Teagan bent down and cupped his face, kissing him urgently.

Chase surged to his feet and wrapped his arms around her, lifting her and swinging her in a full circle. Oblivious to any nearby pedestrians, he kissed her long and deep, claiming her now and forever as his.

"Are you sure about this?" Teagan cried when they at last needed to come up for air. She looked half terrified that he'd change his mind, even as her voice dipped into its familiar flirtatious tones. "I can't promise that I'll settle down and be a proper Charleston wife."

He dusted a kiss across her forehead. "Do you even know what that entails?"

"Supporting my handsome, accomplished husband and everything he does." Her imitation of his mother was spot-on.

"That goes both ways, you know. I fully intend to support my ambitious, clever wife in all her endeavors."

"Oh, please don't do that. I need you to keep me on the straight and narrow."

"Don't sell yourself short. I think you've lost your taste for scheming."

"Maybe. But I'm worried that you can take the girl out of New York but you can't take the schemes out of the girl."

"As long as the girl stays in Charleston, I can handle a little scheming."

"But never with you. I might not have told you about Declan, but I've always been honest when it comes to how I feel about you. That at least I can promise will never change."

"Shall we make that part of our vows?"

"I don't see why not. I, Teagan Burns-Watts, solemnly swear to be honest and transparent with you for the rest of my life."

"And I, Chase Love, promise that I will never doubt you again."

Her green eyes sparkled with unshed tears as she said, "That's a pretty big leap of faith."

"It's one I owe you. For too long I ignored my instincts about you and let others fill my head with their opinions. I should've trusted you."

"To be fair, I made a mess of things before you and I met."

"You hadn't yet learned how to trust me," he told her. "I know that's different now."

"That's because of you. You gave me a safe place to land."

"And then I failed you."

"Not failed. You opened my eyes and gave me the motivation to fix all that I'd broken."

He brought the rolled-up paper into her line of view. "I hope this makes your decision to sell the Brookfield Building a little less painful."

Looking utterly mystified, Teagan unrolled the paper and scanned the page. "I don't understand. This is a report from the Landmark Preservation Commission about the Brookfield Building."

Chase's lips curved into a self-satisfied grin. "It's been designated a landmark."

"How?"

"I called Knox and Paul," he explained. "No one knows more about securing landmark designations in Charleston than my business partner. After you mentioned Declan's influence over certain members of New York's Landmark Preservation Commission, Knox connected with a schoolmate of his that is active in New York real estate."

Chase had recognized that he couldn't go to war with Declan unless he knew the playing field, and from everything he'd learned about the property developer, having a half-assed plan in the works would only end in defeat.

"Once we knew the players, I contacted Paul to do some research on them."

A month earlier the cybersecurity specialist had been integral in figuring out who'd been sending the anonymous texts warning Ethan about Teagan's scheming. In addition to preventing cyber threats, Paul was also quite adept at digging up all sorts of information on people. He had a network of private investigators and law enforcement he worked with all across the country.

"He used his connections to figure out what sort of dirty tactics Declan was using to pressure six commissioners to stall the vote on the Brookfield's landmark status." Chase grinned at her. "Once we applied a little pressure of our own, they agreed that the application should be approved. And voilà."

"You saved it," Teagan murmured in delight. "For me."

His heart skipped a beat as her expression grew radiant. She was the only woman for him and he would've done so much more to prove that to her.

"I knew what it meant to you."

"It meant so much." Teagan winced. "I hope you know that I'm eternally grateful for what you did for me and I'm thrilled that it won't be torn down, but the Brookfield Building is my past." She paused and the fierce light in her eyes held him captive. "You and the Calloway house are my future."

Her fervent pledge demonstrated why he adored her.

"I love you." Chase cupped her face in his hands. "I promise you'll never regret your choice."

Bringing his lips to hers, he sealed his vow with an earnest kiss.

When he lifted his head, Teagan whispered, "I am yours, Chase Love, now and forever. Never doubt how much I love you." Then she took his hand and drew him toward the waiting town car. "Now, take me home to Charleston where I belong."

* * * * *

Look for all the novels in the
Sweet Tea and Scandal series

Upstairs Downstairs Baby
Substitute Seduction
Revenge with Benefits
Seductive Secrets
Seduction, Southern Style
The Trouble with Love and Hate

#2923 ONE NIGHT RANCHER

The Carsons of Lone Rock • by Maisey Yates

To buy the property, bar owner Cara Thompson must spend one night at a ghostly hotel and asks her best friend, Jace Carson, to join her. But when forbidden kisses melt into passion, *both* are haunted by their explosive encounter...

#2924 A COWBOY KIND OF THING

Texas Cattleman's Club: The Wedding • by Reese Ryan

Tripp Nobel is convinced Royal, Texas, is perfect for his famous cousin's wedding. But convincing Dionna Reed, the bride's Hollywood best friend...? The wealthy rancher's kisses soon melt her icy shell, but will they be enough to tempt her to take on this cowboy?

#2925 RODEO REBEL

Kingsland Ranch • by Joanne Rock

With a successful bull rider in her bachelor auction, Lauryn Hamilton's horse rescue is sure to benefit. But rodeo star Gavin Kingsley has his devilish, bad boy gaze on *her*. The good girl. The one who's never ruled by reckless passion—until now...

#2926 THE INHERITANCE TEST

by Anne Marsh

Movie star Declan Masterson needs to rehabilitate his playboy image fast to save his inheritance! Partnering with Jane Charlotte—the quintessential "plain jane"—for a charity yacht race is a genius first step. If only there wasn't a captivating woman underneath Jane's straightlaced exterior...

#2927 BILLIONAIRE FAKE OUT

The Image Project • by Katherine Garbera

Paisley Campbell just learned her lover is a famous Hollywood A-lister... and she's expecting his baby! Sean O'Neill knows he's been living on borrowed time by keeping his identity secret. Can he convince her that everything they shared was not just a celebrity stunt?

#2928 A GAME OF SECRETS

The Eddington Heirs • by Zuri Day

CEO Jake Eddington was charged with protecting his friend's beautiful sister from players and users. And he knows *he* should resist their chemistry too...but socialite Sasha McDowell is too captivating to ignore—even if their tryst ignites a scandal...

Get 4 FREE REWARDS!

We'll send you 2 FREE Books plus 2 FREE Mystery Gifts.

FREE Value Over **$20**

Both the **Harlequin® Desire** and **Harlequin Presents®** series feature compelling novels filled with passion, sensuality and intriguing scandals.

YES! Please send me 2 FREE novels from the Harlequin Desire or Harlequin Presents series and my 2 FREE gifts (gifts are worth about $10 retail). After receiving them, if I don't wish to receive any more books, I can return the shipping statement marked "cancel." If I don't cancel, I will receive 6 brand-new Harlequin Presents Larger-Print books every month and be billed just $6.30 each in the U.S. or $6.49 each in Canada, a savings of at least 10% off the cover price, or 6 Harlequin Desire books every month and be billed just $5.05 each in the U.S. or $5.74 each in Canada, a savings of at least 12% off the cover price. It's quite a bargain! Shipping and handling is just 50¢ per book in the U.S. and $1.25 per book in Canada.* I understand that accepting the 2 free books and gifts places me under no obligation to buy anything. I can always return a shipment and cancel at any time by calling the number below. The free books and gifts are mine to keep no matter what I decide.

Choose one: ☐ **Harlequin Desire**
(225/326 HDN GRJ7)

☐ **Harlequin Presents Larger-Print**
(176/376 HDN GRJ7)

Name (please print)

Address   Apt. #

City   State/Province   Zip/Postal Code

Email: Please check this box ☐ if you would like to receive newsletters and promotional emails from Harlequin Enterprises ULC and its affiliates. You can unsubscribe anytime.

Mail to the **Harlequin Reader Service:**
IN U.S.A.: P.O. Box 1341, Buffalo, NY 14240-8531
IN CANADA: P.O. Box 603, Fort Erie, Ontario L2A 5X3

Want to try 2 free books from another series! Call 1-800-873-8635 or visit www.ReaderService.com.

*Terms and prices subject to change without notice. Prices do not include sales taxes, which will be charged (if applicable) based on your state or country of residence. Canadian residents will be charged applicable taxes. Offer not valid in Quebec. This offer is limited to one order per household. Books received may not be as shown. Not valid for current subscribers to the Harlequin Presents or Harlequin Desire series. All orders subject to approval. Credit or debit balances in a customer's account(s) may be offset by any other outstanding balance owed by or to the customer. Please allow 4 to 6 weeks for delivery. Offer available while quantities last.

Your Privacy—Your information is being collected by Harlequin Enterprises ULC, operating as Harlequin Reader Service. For a complete summary of the information we collect, how we use this information and to whom it is disclosed, please visit our privacy notice located at corporate.harlequin.com/privacy-notice. From time to time we may also exchange your personal information with reputable third parties. If you wish to opt out of this sharing of your personal information, please visit readerservice.com/consumerschoice or call 1-800-873-8635. **Notice to California Residents**—Under California law, you have specific rights to control and access your data. For more information on these rights and how to exercise them, visit corporate.harlequin.com/california-privacy.

HDHP22R3

HARLEQUIN
PLUS

Announcing a **BRAND-NEW** multimedia subscription service for romance fans like you!

Read, Watch and Play.

Experience the easiest way to get the romance content you crave.

Start your **FREE 7 DAY TRIAL** at www.harlequinplus.com/freetrial.

She will not be unfaithful, she would never be unfaith-
to Elliott, who she loves with all her heart and soul. But
self-esteem, already so fragile, can treasure this eve-
g, this gentle chemistry, this feeling of someone as gor-
ous as Matt being interested in her, for years to come.
And what would be the harm?

e really had fun tonight." Gabby sighs, a couple of
irs later. Coffee became Irish coffee, and she is aware
t her sobriety said goodbye a very long time ago.

"For the record," Matt says, "I don't make a habit of
ing at bars and flirting with lovely looking ladies. Es-
cially when I'm traveling for work. You have made a
·ing business trip completely delightful."

Gabby says nothing, too busy twisting the words he
t used over and over in his mind. "Lovely looking!"
lirting!" I wasn't imagining it!

"I'll have them call you a cab." He doesn't move.

There is no one else in the hotel lounge. It is now
e early hours of the morning. One receptionist is there,
e lights dim.

Matt and Gabby stare at each other, as Gabby wills her-
f to move, to get up, to get out and go home before . . .
fore it's too late. But she can't move, her heart is pound-
·, an unfamiliar heat coursing through her body, and she
ows she has to go, but she can't do anything other than
re into the eyes of this man as she lets out a deep sigh.

"Why are all the women I like unavailable?" he whis-
rs, as Gabby's heart threatens to jump out of her body.
e doesn't know what to say. She wants to leave, knows
e has to leave, but oh, how she wants to stay.

"I should go." Her voice is a whisper, and mustering
the strength she can manage she reluctantly climbs to
r feet.